KU-711-700

# Julia Green says:

When I'd finished Blue Moon, my first novel, Mia was still vividly present in my mind. I knew there was much more to say about her, and of course the new baby.

I wanted to say something about being a mother: how hard it is, how important, how life-changing, whatever age you are. And I wanted to show the magic, the miracle, that all babies are.

The challenge for Mia is to love and look after her own baby, but not to give up on her own life. That's one of the real challenges for all mothers, I think, balancing those two things. You have to have your own dreams, find your own wings.

Julia Green lives in Bath with her partner and two children. She lectures part-time in English and creative writing, leads writing workshops for adults and young people, and works as a home-tutor for children who are not attending school.

*Books by Julia Green*

**BABY BLUE**
**BLUE MOON**

# Julia Green

# baby Blue

PUFFIN

PUFFIN BOOKS

Published by the Penguin Group
Penguin Books Ltd, 80 Strand, London WC2R 0RL, England
Penguin Group (USA), Inc., 375 Hudson Street, New York, New York 10014, USA
Penguin Books Australia Ltd, 250 Camberwell Road, Camberwell, Victoria 3124, Australia
Penguin Books Canada Ltd, 10 Alcorn Avenue, Toronto, Ontario, Canada M4V 3B2
Penguin Books India (P) Ltd, 11 Community Centre, Panchsheel Park, New Delhi – 110 017, India
Penguin Books (NZ) Ltd, Cnr Rosedale and Airborne Roads, Albany, Auckland, New Zealand
Penguin Books (South Africa) (Pty) Ltd, 24 Sturdee Avenue, Rosebank 2196, South Africa

Penguin Books Ltd, Registered Offices: 80 Strand, London WC2R 0RL, England

www.penguin.com

First published 2004
4

Copyright © Julia Green, 2004
Excerpt of 'Poem to my Daughter' © Anne Stevenson,
*The Collected Poems 1955–1995*, Bloodaxe Books, 2000,
has been reproduced by kind permission of the publisher.
All rights reserved

The moral right of the author has been asserted

Set in 11.5/16 pt Adobe Sabon
Typeset by Rowland Phototypesetting Ltd, Bury St Edmunds, Suffolk

Made and printed in England by Clays Ltd, St Ives plc

Except in the United States of America, this book is sold subject to the condition
that it shall not, by way of trade or otherwise, be lent, re-sold, hired out, or otherwise
circulated without the publisher's prior consent in any form of binding or cover other
than that in which it is published and without a similar condition including
this condition being imposed on the subsequent purchaser

British Library Cataloguing in Publication Data
A CIP catalogue record for this book is available from the British Library

ISBN 0–141–31679–9

*For my family*

The child,
tiny and alone, creates the mother.

*from 'Poem to my Daughter'*
*by Anne Stevenson*

## CHAPTER ONE

*W*hite walls, white ceiling, white starched sheets, white blanket, like a cot blanket. Mia lies completely still, eyes open. Through the tall window she can see blue sky divided into nine neat squares – the fresh-rinsed blue of a sky after rain. It's very early in the morning, she can tell even without looking at her watch. Which is where? Someone must have brought all her things up for her and put them in the bedside locker. She is marooned in this too-high bed, the sheet stretched taut across her aching body, the sides tucked in under the mattress so that she can hardly move. She can't think how she got here.

She shifts gingerly and feels the blood rushing into her imprisoned limbs; her numbed feet and hands prickle and throb back to life. Washed up, scoured out like a shell, that's her. Empty. Bone-clean.

It's as if she's just arrived at a completely new destination. The sole survivor of a terrible storm, newly washed up on an island shore.

Her mouth is parched. She pushes herself up against the pile of pillows to reach the water jug and glass someone has left for her on the bedside cabinet. A spasm of pain zigzags down her stomach and into her thighs.

Why have they put her in here, by herself?

*By herself.*

Her belly lurches.

At the foot of the bed, there's a plastic transparent crib like a fish tank. A white cot blanket.

*They've taken him away already, even though I said I didn't want him to go to the nursery. 'You need your sleep,' they said, but I said, 'No, I want him here with me all the time.' They've waited for me to sleep and they've come and stolen him away because they think I can't look after him. They don't trust me. They want him for themselves, to coo over and fuss and say how beautiful he is, with his tuft of dark seaweed hair and his deep blue eyes and his starfish hands. He's too good for me. Too sweet and perfect.*

The white blanket in the cot stirred; a tiny, crinkled arm pushed against it. Relief flooded through Mia. And terror. It was all up to her now. She swivelled round and eased herself down on to the floor, felt the cool lino on her bare feet, and steadied herself with one hand on the bed as she crept round to the crib. Her legs shook and her belly tightened with pain, an echo of the night's effort. With her free hand she pulled the fish-tank crib round to the side of the bed so she could see properly inside.

There he was! The shock, a second time, to see him! This utterly strange, yet utterly familiar little person with his own hair and eyes and ears and baby-bird mouth.

'Hello, you,' Mia whispered into the crib.

She half wanted to scoop him up and nuzzle her face into his, snuffle his skin. Half didn't dare.

She'd slept, and he'd slept, for nearly five hours. It was all a miracle.

Mia drifted in and out of sleep.

Remembered.

They called it *labour*, the work of the body getting ready for birth. At first the contractions of the womb had felt like elastic bands round her body, getting tighter and tighter and squeezing the breath out. Rings of pain, tightening and squeezing her belly. It was a bit like surfing, riding the waves of pain, seeing them coming, judging how to take them, knowing you could do it, only gradually getting more tired. Then the waves started getting bigger, and too close to each other, one and the next and the next relentlessly on and on, with the breaks getting smaller and no time to catch your breath before the next one hit and went over your head. That had been terrible, that bit. Everything dark and full of panic, a long descent like drowning, feeling as if you were being scraped over the stones at the bottom of the beach and finally left torn and bloody and sick with fear. But alive.

She had thought she might die, but she hadn't. And he hadn't either. Feeling his body sort of slither and tumble out between her legs, too quick, while someone was still yelling at her not to push, to *breathe*. That was giving birth.

Hot, and sweaty, and bloody, and *animal*. Mia shuddered now at the thought of her nakedness in front of strangers. She was so glad it had happened so fast, that no one from her family had been in the room. Most other women had *husbands*, or *partners*, of course. Imagine, having Will there. He'd have died of shock. Blood and gore in a film: that was a different matter. But not the real thing. He'd never have handled that.

Dad's face when he came in after it was all over. *A boy!* For once, he'd had no words. Tears were running down his cheeks. For once, for the first time ever, Mia felt she had done something to make him pleased with her. The gift of a boy-child.

There was a light tap at the door. It opened; a young nurse smiled wearily at Mia.

'You're awake, then? I popped in earlier but you were sound asleep.' She took Mia's temperature, lightly placed two cool fingers on her pulse and watched the seconds tick round on the watch pinned to her pocket.

'OK? Normal. No infection. Good. Baby fed yet? Changed his nappy? Poo or wee?'

Mia shook her head.

'Call someone to help you do the first nappy. You brought some in? Yes?'

Mia stared back, blank.

'Why don't you go and have a shower while you can? You can collect breakfast from the day room any time after seven.'

The nurse walked over to the window and looked out across the car park. Mia watched her. How old was she? Twenty? A student nurse? Mia's sister Laura was about the same age.

A shower would be good. Her hair was matted with sweat and her skin felt like rubber. She was hungry, too. She'd thought someone would bring her a tray, or at least tea, while she was still in bed, not that she'd have to go and find it for herself. She couldn't imagine walking as far as the day room. What should she do with the baby? Was it safe to leave him?

The young nurse turned back towards Mia. 'You're

lucky they put you in a single room. All the mothers and babies in the eight-bed rooms wake each other up all night. No one gets any sleep. That's why they end up putting the babies in the nursery.'

'What will happen if he wakes up while I'm in the shower?'

The nurse laughed. 'Oh, he'll be all right. He'll have to get used to it, won't he? I'll watch him for you if you like. I'm on till seven, then it's the day shift.'

Mia looked protectively towards her tiny sleeping son. But she needed a shower badly.

The moment she opened the bathroom door after her shower she could hear the thin wail of a baby. Hers? The nurse was busy talking on the phone at the main desk. *So much for looking after him!* Mia stumbled along the corridor, tying the hospital dressing gown round her, back to her single room.

His face was steamy red, his eyes squeezed shut in anguish and misery. Mia's whole body went hot. She'd have to pick him up. His body felt stiff and awkward as she tried to scoop him out of the crib. His legs and arms jerked out as she unwrapped the blanket, his back arched away from her. *He doesn't know me. He doesn't know I'm his mother – he can tell I'm scared.*

Mia bit her lip as she forced herself to wrap him

back up and lift him close to her body. There was a wild moment of struggle as she tried to settle him close in against her, then suddenly the crying stopped and his mouth started to gape and rootle against her, searching for her breast. He screwed his face up in disappointment again as he found only the rough towelling dressing gown, opened his mouth to howl. Just in time Mia untied the cord and his mouth sensed skin, warm breast. It felt so weird, his whole mouth pulling fiercely at her nipple. It began to hurt, he wasn't latched on properly, but she couldn't bear to get him off and properly positioned again, and so she kept on biting her lip and let this new pain join the others in her body.

'I thought I heard something.' The tired nurse stood in the doorway.

The baby's head jerked away and he butted against Mia's chest as he began to wail.

'You want to hold his head for him, he can't support it yet. With your hand. And get him properly latched on or you'll get blisters and cracks in your nipples and then you'll be putting him on the bottle before you know what you're doing. Look, let me show you.'

She pulled one of the pillows from behind Mia and placed it on her lap, to raise the baby up higher. Then she manoeuvred him into position.

'There. You want to see that his whole mouth goes round like that. That's on properly now. See? He's getting something now. Colostrum, until your milk comes through properly. It's full of goodness. Well done! You'll be all right now. Got to go. Ring your buzzer if you want someone. Don't forget about breakfast.'

Tears prickled in Mia's eyes. It was already too hard. He was only seven hours old. What on earth had made her feel she could do this by herself? The baby sucked contentedly while Mia sobbed into his hair.

## CHAPTER TWO

'*M*ia? Wasn't sure if you were awake. Didn't want to disturb you two.'

Dad hovered at the door, a huge bunch of white lilac held awkwardly in one hand.

Mia tried to smile. 'Flowers.'

'From the garden. For you. And him. How's he doing?'

'OK. What's the time?'

'Twelve-ish.'

*Don't wake up. Please.* If he woke up he'd cry and then she'd have to feed him, and how could she possibly do that with her dad looking? Mia went hot and sweaty at the thought, and, as if on cue, the baby started to whimper.

'Shall I pick him up for you?' Dad leaped over enthusiastically to the crib and started clucking at the baby.

'Leave him be, Dad. Wait.'

He might just settle back to sleep. *Please, Baby. Not now.*

The whimpering went up a level, from a sort of mewing to an open-mouthed wail.

'Go on, then, pick him up.' She watched him lean over the crib.

'It's OK, little fella.'

The baby stopped crying to listen to the unfamiliar voice and in that second Dad had scooped him up. He cradled the tiny baby against his chest for a moment. His face had gone soft, smoothed out with tenderness.

'Here you are, then. Here's your mum.'

Dad carefully laid the baby in Mia's arms. Her face went red and hot again. The baby started to cry louder.

'I'll go and get a vase or something for the flowers while you sort him out.' Dad closed the door gently, tactfully, behind him.

*Good.* Mia let out a huge sigh. She lifted up her T-shirt and let the baby find her breast. It didn't look like hers at all; it was swollen and lumpy-looking and criss-crossed with blue veins. Round the nipples the skin was all brown and peculiar. It was supposed to look like this, apparently. The leaflet the nurse had left for her on the table said it would get even worse when her milk came in. You were supposed to have something called a nursing bra in a mega-huge size to support your breasts, but she hadn't got one. She'd rather die than wear the ones she and her friend Becky had looked at a few weeks ago.

The baby wailed in despair for a second, his head frantically bobbing about until she held it for him and steered him towards her breast. His mouth opened up round her nipple and a sharp pain shot through her belly, but he was on now, starting to suck noisily. *Greedy little pig.*

Once the baby was latched on properly, she could let her T-shirt flop back down and no one could really see anything.

The nurses were pleased with her for having a go at breastfeeding. 'Most girls your age don't. But it's so much better for the baby if you can. Better for you, too. Helps you bond.'

It felt so weird. *Hurry up*, she willed him. *Finish before Dad gets back.*

The baby seemed to know what she was thinking. He stopped sucking and let the nipple drop, and then he made a funny drizzling, miserable sound. He turned his face away when she tried to help him back on. His body went stiff in her hands. Just as the door opened he started to bawl.

Dad followed meekly behind a nurse who bore the vase of garden flowers before her like a bridal bouquet. She set them on the windowsill.

'Aren't they lovely? Such a beautiful scent! And from your garden! Lucky you!' She smiled too generously at Dad, who simpered back.

*Typical*, Mia thought. *Even in here he's at it.*

'Now what's all that noise about?' The nurse looked accusingly at Mia. 'Have you winded him after feeding?' She took the baby from her without even asking and put him over her shoulder, patting his back as she walked around the tiny room with him.

Mia had seen people do that with babies, to make them burp up wind. But she was sure the nurse was patting him much too hard: his little face was peeping at Mia over her starched shoulder, wide-eyed and terrified. He was so very small. So crumpled and defeated-looking.

*Why can't they all go away and leave us alone?*

'How are you, love? Can I get you anything?'

Dad's gentle voice was enough to push Mia over the edge. She started to cry, couldn't seem to stop. Embarrassed, he shuffled through his pocket for a tissue, but of course there wasn't one. Balancing the baby with one hand, with the other Super Nurse passed him a box of tissues from the trolley and smiled at him.

'Touch of the baby blues. Perfectly normal, it's just her hormones,' she explained in her patronizing voice.

Dad smiled back weakly and patted Mia's back as if she'd got wind, too.

The baby had gone quiet. The nurse laid him back in the crib. 'There you are. He's fine now. Must get on.'

Mia and Dad listened to the efficient squeak of her shoes as she disappeared back along the corridor. He looked at Mia and shrugged.

'Dreadful woman! Poor you. Hope they're not all like that. You all right now?'

Mia nodded, sniffed.

'Shall I bring you some food when I come back later? What would you like? I know your mother was always hungry after having a baby, and hospital food isn't up to much.'

'Tuna fish sandwiches. Crisps. Bananas.'

'Anything else?'

'Disposable nappies. I was supposed to bring some in with me.'

He grinned. 'Better than when you were born. We used those terry-towelling nappies in the hospital. Always worrying about the pin!'

Dad wandered round the small room, picking up the chart at the foot of the bed to look at it, fiddling with the pots of cream on the trolley. 'I can't stay long. You have a bit of a rest, yes? Before the other visitors arrive. Becky wants to come after school this afternoon, and your mother's driving from Bristol this evening, probably. We managed to phone Kate in Greece; she sends her love. Says it's funny to think she's an auntie. I know what she means. Can't believe I'm a grandfather!'

And Mia a mother. At sixteen. Neither of them said it, but the thought hovered in the air anyway.

'It's nice they've put you here, in a single room. More private. Though it's a bit lonely ... Still, it's not for long. A couple of days, the nurse said. Till you've got the feeding sorted ...' His voice trailed off. 'I'll let you sleep, shall I? See you later, then, love.'

She knew that anxious look as he went out of the door. *Is she going to manage this? Is she responsible enough? Has she made a terrible mistake?*

The sun had moved higher in the sky; it reflected off the white walls, flooded the room with warmth. The white lilac shimmered on the windowsill. Already, some of the tiny flowers had dropped on to the sill shedding a fine dust of pollen. A trolley rattled and creaked along a corridor, voices and laughter drifted from the main desk at the nurses' station, telephones rang.

Mia felt utterly alone. Ached with it. Why did the nurses keep insisting she put the baby back in the crib? She clambered painfully out of bed again. He was lying wide-eyed in the crib, awake but still. *Little Bean*. That's what she'd called him all through her pregnancy. *Can't call you that any more. Have to find you a name.*

'Come here, little one,' she whispered to him, feeling silly, not wanting anyone to hear. Gritting her teeth, she eased one hand under him and carefully picked him up, wrapping the blanket round him tightly, like she'd seen the nurses do. 'There. That's better, isn't it?'

It had been easier that time, getting him out of the stupid crib. She wasn't quite so scared of dropping him. And he hadn't cried, or jerked out his arms in shock and terror.

She shuffled to the window, the baby held close in her arms. There was a world still out there, then; things happening, life carrying on. Outside, everything looked the same. It seemed surprising, somehow. She'd just had a baby, her, Mia, and no one out there knew anything about it! Men from a refuse lorry were emptying bins at the side of the hospital, joking and carrying on as normal. While up here, on the fifth floor, Princess Diana Maternity Wing, Ashton General, she was holding her newborn son in her arms.

She was overwhelmed with a longing to be outside,

15

breathing fresh spring air, feeling the sun on her skin. It was much too hot in the ward, the air stale, as if it had been being breathed in and out by too many people. *Like on a plane*, Mia thought. She closed her eyes a second. Held on to the image of a sleek silver aeroplane high in a pale blue sky, sun reflecting off the wings. High up, free, going somewhere.

The baby blinked and closed his eyes in the dazzling sunlight.

She spoke to him in her head, as she had done when he was still inside her, knowing he could somehow hear her and understand. *I'll get you out of here soon. Don't you worry, Baby.*

## CHAPTER THREE

'He's *amazing*, Mia! Look at his little tiny fingernails. And his ears like shells. Oh, he's just so sweet!' Becky stood by the crib, gazing at the sleeping baby. She'd come here straight from school. Couldn't wait to see the baby, after Mia's dad had phoned that morning. And her, of course.

Mia saw him again through Becky's eyes. He did look sweet right now: his dark hair fluffed out on the white sheet, the curve of his cheek, strawberry mouth. Not the fierce, red-faced angry little thing she had been struggling with all afternoon. She was exhausted. It was ten to four.

'Everyone else is dead envious, but your dad said just me. I've brought my camera –'

'No,' Mia interrupted her. 'Please, no pictures. Not yet.'

Becky looked surprised. 'Why not?'

'I don't – it doesn't feel right. I don't like the flash – and – tomorrow, maybe. He's just too new.'

'What's he wearing? I've brought him this, only I didn't realize he'd be so small.' Becky fished out a parcel and started unwrapping the tissue. It was a turquoise Babygro, with purple sea horses swimming between strands of green seaweed. 'I thought it'd go with your room at home.'

'It's lovely, Becks. Thanks. He's still in the hospital thing – a sort of gown, with ties at the back. It's not very nice.'

'Shall we change him, then? When he wakes up?'

'Oh. I dunno. I'm not sure if he'll like being undressed.'

She couldn't imagine how they could possibly take his tiny arms out of the sleeves and put them into new clothes; all that messing him around. He'd shriek and go stiff, like he did with the nappy. He didn't seem to like being unwrapped. Becky would see how badly she was doing already. For Becky, though, it was all still a wonderful game, Mia realized. She'd already redecorated Mia's room with her – she'd redesigned it for her GCSE project. She'd probably get an A, what with all the drawings and fabric samples and the photographs step-by-step of the transformation. And it was lovely. Now she was starting on his clothes. Like he was a doll or something.

'And this is for you, because we didn't get very far

with our list for boys, did we? And I thought it might help.'

Mia unwrapped a small book from the paper bag. *The Pocket Reference Guide to Babies' Names*. A pink-cheeked baby in a pink dress smiled out from the shiny cover.

'Thanks.'

'Shall we look now? Together?'

She shook her head. 'He's too small. I mean, I don't know who he is yet. Oh, I don't know.'

She wouldn't let Becky see her cry. She wouldn't.

Becky looked disappointed about the names; she'd even brought a pen and some paper, so they could get started on a new list of names for boys. She sat down on the bed.

'Tomorrow, maybe? Will you still be here? When can you go home?'

'I'm not sure. They want me to stay in a couple of days.'

'Anyway, tell me everything. Did it hurt a lot? How did you know it was happening? What was it like?'

Mia propped herself further up on the pillows. She groaned as she moved her legs.

'Are you hurting now?'

'Yes. A bit. When I move.'

'Did you have to have stitches? My mum says that's the pits, worse even than the birth.'

'No, but it still hurts.'

'I can imagine. Well, I can't really, but sort of. Poor you! But look! A real baby! It's so incredible! Go on, tell me about it.'

'Well – it's like – well, it does hurt, lots. I mean, look at the size of him. That's what had to come out of me! That head. But it was quick. The midwife person said I was lucky, being young and that. There were women in the delivery room who'd been there all day and all night, but I just turned up at ten or something and he was born just after midnight. It was really messy, and the baby looked weird at first, his head was a funny shape. And I made such a noise!'

Already, Becky wasn't really listening. She was back peering at the baby, willing him to wake up so she could see him properly and hold him. 'I can't believe it! A real baby! So, so cute! Wait till my mum sees him. She'll go all gooey. She's been buying you stuff. She's taking a heap of it round to your place this afternoon, and after your dad phoned this morning she started cooking extra so he can put it in the freezer for you and him. He said no, but she's doing it anyway.'

'What kind of stuff?'

'What?'

'What stuff has your mum been buying?'

'Oh, nappies and cotton wool and stuff, and these

cute little vests with poppers that you do up under their bum, and a creamy blanket for that basket thing you've got.'

'But I've got everything already.'

'She's trying to be helpful, Mia. Don't go all moody on me now.'

'I'm not.'

'Good.'

Mia leaned back against the pillows. Everything was too bright in the room. Becky's voice seemed too loud. She closed her eyes briefly. Dad should be back soon with stuff for her. Decent food, for one thing. She was starving. She'd never made it to breakfast, and the hospital lunch was so disgusting she'd hardly eaten anything.

Becky's voice chattered away: '. . . so excited. They all wanted to come but I said not yet, they wouldn't let us all in at once. Just as well, cos they nearly didn't let me in till I said I was family.'

'What?'

'I said I was part of your family. It's families only for visiting this afternoon. And after seven p.m. it's husbands and partners only!'

Dust floated along the wedges of sunlight. It was much too warm in here. Made her sleepy and stupid and sad.

'Oh, I nearly forgot, I've got something else for

you.' Becky pulled out a blue envelope from her school rucksack. Mia's name was written on the front in Becky's neat round script.

She leaned forwards to open it. Her first baby card. *Congratulations!* it said. Most of the Year Eleven group had signed it. Siobhan, Ali, Liam, Matt, Rob, even people she didn't know very well. And her old tutor, Miss Blackman. There were kisses. Tasha had drawn a little heart. *Where's his name? The only one that matters?* She scanned the names again, looking for Will, in case she'd missed him. But no. It wasn't anywhere.

'Thanks. Did you organize it?' Her voice was bleak.

'Yes. Everyone's really pleased for you. Even Miss Blackman went all soft.'

'She can bog off.'

'Well, I know.'

'She's probably there in my house right now, making the most of it because I'm stuck in here.'

Becky sighed. 'Oh, Mia. She's not so bad. And your dad's happy. At least it keeps him off your back.'

'She'll be wanting a baby next.'

Becky giggled. 'And then your baby would be her baby's uncle or something.'

'Not uncle. Grandson or half-brother or – oh, I don't know – it's all ridiculous.'

A rustling, stirring sound from the crib silenced

them both. Mia crawled down to the foot of her bed and pulled the crib closer. There he was again. That strawberry mouth beginning to work, opening and closing, searching for her, that sound like a kitten's mew. She reached in and lifted him out. His body felt warm, quivering against hers.

'Oh, look! He's so small. Oh, my God, Mia!' Becky's eyes had filled with tears. She saw it too; how vulnerable and afraid and fragile he was, how much he needed. He wasn't like a baby doll at all.

Mia cuddled him into her chest. Perhaps he didn't need a feed. Not again. Not yet. While she was looking at his little face, he opened his eyes wide open and stared back.

Becky edged closer. She sat behind Mia on the bed, looking over her shoulder at the baby's face.

'He's got blue eyes. Like Will.' The words escaped from her mouth; too late to pull them back.

Mia's eyes stung. 'All white babies have blue eyes. They don't stay like that. He's got dark hair like me.' Her voice was fierce. 'I'm going to feed him now. Can you go, so he doesn't get distracted? I can't do it if you're watching.'

Becky looked hurt. 'OK. Sorry. I'll come again tomorrow, shall I?'

Mia nodded without looking up.

Becky hesitated. 'Mia? I'm sorry – Will – he didn't

sign the card because he wasn't in school. I know you were looking for his name.'

'It's not your fault. It doesn't matter.'

'See you tomorrow, then?'

'Yes. Thanks, Becks.'

Mia waited for the door to close, sighed, lifted up her T-shirt for the next feed. *Start on the other side next time*, the nurse had said. *Make sure you use both breasts*. She had to turn him round; it felt even more difficult. He struggled, and arched, and cried. Mia fixed all her attention on the baby. She wouldn't think about Will now. She winced as the baby's mouth moved tighter on her nipple.

## CHAPTER FOUR

She'd lost all sense of time. It was evening, but if someone had told her it was the next day, or the one after that, she would have believed them. Dad walked round the small room, the baby pressed against his shoulder. The baby had stopped crying now and opened his eyes. Mia watched his dark head bobbing against Dad's linen shirt. A pale curdy dribble of milk stiffened on the blue fabric.

'So have you decided yet? On a name?' Mum picked up the little book from the bedside cabinet and leafed through the pages.

It was as if they couldn't believe in the baby till he had a name. In her head she'd started to call him Birdy. She'd whispered it in his ear, to see what he did. Nothing. He was so tiny and fragile in his body, but she saw already how he wasn't really like that at all inside. He knew who he was. He wasn't her, he was someone else. Separate. It was just that she couldn't work out who yet. She was afraid of giving him the wrong name, as if the name would tie him down or make him someone else.

'What about a family name? My dad was Jacob.' Mum flipped through the Js and started reading aloud what it said. ' "From the Hebrew meaning 'deceiver' or 'supplanter'." Maybe not!' She laughed. 'It's easier with girls, somehow. We just *knew* with you three – Laura, Kate, Mia. Laura sends her love, by the way. She's sorry she couldn't get away; an essay to finish or something. She's sending a card.'

While Mum nattered on and on, Mia's mind drifted. She'd already looked up her own name. *Italian for 'my', and a version of Mary – from the Hebrew name Miriam, meaning 'sea of bitterness', or 'O child of our wishes', or from the Latin* stella maris, *meaning 'star of the sea'.*

Mum and Dad had been here together for nearly an hour. Without arguing, either. They'd arrived together, Mum smart and sexy in a black linen suit, her hair cut sleek and short, and both had hugged Mia, and then each held the baby in turn, and both cried, and then laughed about being grandparents. Mia ate the sandwiches Dad had brought with him, and Mum arranged her shop-bought bouquet of white lilies on the windowsill, and then Mia dozed off again until the baby started crying.

Dad seemed to be able to settle him so much more easily than her.

A nurse put her head round the door. 'End of visiting time ten minutes ago! New mums need lots of rest!' She hovered, waiting till she saw them gathering up their things to leave before she went to shoo other errant visitors off the premises.

Mum grimaced. 'Oh dear. Such awful places, hospitals, aren't they? We'd better do what we're told. But it's not long now and you can come home, love.'

For a second Mia imagined what it would be like, to 'come home' to both Mum and Dad in the old house in Whitecross. But it was just a slip of the tongue; Mum's home was in Bristol, with Bryan, miles away. Dad would be there, though. She could probably go home tomorrow, the nurse said, all being well.

They both hugged her goodbye. She was awkward, felt her own body go stiff, just like Birdy's did. She stood at the doorway to watch them walk down the corridor; they turned and waved once. She felt more lonely than ever when they'd gone. She stayed there, watching the other late visitors leaving the ward. The fathers. Husbands and partners. Finally, when the corridors were empty again, she went back into her room and stood at the window.

Dark outside. Headlights from cars manoeuvring in the car park below. Blue flashing lights, siren, as an ambulance raced in. A flurry of activity. Someone was carried in on a stretcher. An aeroplane, lights winking. From the tree outside her window, a sudden squawking and twittering of hundreds of roosting starlings. The night settled down.

Squeaky shoes, rattling trolley. Doors slammed. Voices.

'Hot drink, dear?' A broad woman squeezed into a checked uniform smiled from the open doorway.

Mia shook her head.

'Sure? It'll help you sleep, my darling.'

'No thanks.' Mia was worn out from so much politeness. Longed to be anywhere but here.

At nine thirty the nurse pushed round the medicine trolley, offering painkillers and sleeping tablets. 'Shall we take baby to the nursery tonight? You look tired out.'

'No. I want him with me.'

'Well, you can always change your mind. Give the night staff something to do!' She laughed bitterly. 'I'm off duty now. Should have gone half an hour ago but the agency nurses don't know where anything is. See you tomorrow.'

The baby still slept.

Mia went back to her seat at the window.

Most of the lights had gone from the car park. The sky looked vast and black. No stars. Her eye caught a movement from near the tree; someone was walking along the footpath at the base of the new block. The figure stopped. She stared.

The dark shape of someone looking up at the windows. Could it be? She looked again. It was a young man, but she couldn't see his face properly in the shadow. Perhaps it was. Perhaps he couldn't keep away after all. Very gently, she picked up the sleeping baby, still wrapped in his blanket, and carried him back with her to the window, held him up against her shoulder like Dad had done earlier. Anyone looking up would see them there, together, wouldn't they? Framed in the light at the window. Anyone who wanted to. When she looked down again she couldn't see him any more. Perhaps there hadn't been anyone there after all.

She laid the baby back in the crib without him waking.

Ten o'clock. Almost the end of the day.

The longest day ever.

## CHAPTER FIVE

*H*e woke every two hours. Dizzy with exhaustion, Mia took him into the bed with her at four in the morning, and he settled at last into a deeper sort of sleep and she half dozed, her arms round him, terrified that he would roll out of the too-high bed on to the hard floor. At six one of the agency nurses in a dark blue uniform came tutting into the room, furious with Mia for breaking the rules. Her loud voice woke the baby.

'He could have rolled out on to the floor and cracked his skull from that height!'

Mia winced, then stiffened with anger as the nurse went on and on about *insurance* and *not allowed* and *that's what the crib is for.*

'Can't you see that poor baby's desperate for some sleep, instead of being cuddled all night? No wonder he's crying.'

How dare she! It was she who'd woken him up, made him cry in the first place. 'Piss off!' Mia muttered.

'I beg your pardon?'

She'd heard all right. Mia had gone too far this time. The baby's shrieks radiated out from the small room into the corridor as far as the nurses' station, bringing another nurse – the young one who'd been on duty yesterday – barging into her room. *They'd been expecting trouble. They knew she wouldn't be able to do it, not at her age.* Mia could imagine the gossip.

This one was overly bright and cheerful. 'Morning, Mia! Had some sleep? He's got a good pair of lungs on him! Why don't you let us take Baby for a while and you have some more rest? It won't do him any harm.' She talked loudly, as if Mia might be deaf. Or stupid.

Mia imagined the two nurses were sending warning signals to each other. That look. The shrug of the shoulders. False smiles.

'Please. I just want to be left alone. I'm fine.'

She imagined them writing on her notes. *Query: not coping? Teenage mum appears rather upset and anxious. Call in hospital counsellor? Keep in for observation.*

For now, however, they did as she said, leaving her alone. They left the door ajar. She could hear voices from the corridor, although not the actual words.

The baby's cheeks were red-hot. He was crying

without tears; his eyes squeezed tight, as if he couldn't bear to see anything, to be here in this room. His hands were little tight fists, knocking against the side of the plastic crib. Mia forced herself to take deep breaths, calm herself down. She braced herself, preparing to scoop him up out of the crib, waiting for the jerking arms and the shrieks of protest at being unwrapped. Each time, she was afraid that she would drop him.

'It's OK, little Birdy. Not long and I'll get us out of here,' she whispered into his shell ear as she lifted him up, and as if by magic he opened his eyes and the crying stopped. She could hardly believe it! It was as if he'd heard her, believed her! Grateful, she pushed her face against his, nuzzled him. His mouth tried to catch hold of her nose to suck, and she smiled. It tickled.

Suddenly it felt a bit easier to settle him on the pillow on her lap and get him positioned right to feed. Left breast first this time. She relaxed; he sucked. They settled down together.

Ten minutes later, he was still hungry. She carefully turned him round, so he could start on the other side, the right breast.

Mia traced her finger over his cheeks. She noticed a cluster of tiny spots on his nose, and in the middle of his top lip a sort of blister. What did that mean?

What was she doing wrong now? Her stomach fluttered with panic again. *It's too hard. I know nothing. I've never even held a newborn baby before, and now they expect me to do everything.*

He went on sucking, eyes closed. She'd have to ask someone – Dad or Mum, not those horrible nurses.

Mia's skin prickled. She sensed a shadow at the door. Someone checking up on her, no doubt. Looking for an excuse to whip the baby away. She glanced up at the small window in the door, expecting to see the white cap and professional smile of one of the nurses. Wrong.

Messed-up golden hair. Tense, frowning sixteen-year-old boy's face.

She almost dropped the baby.

Will sidled in through the doorway and stood with his back to it.

'No one saw. I just walked in. Unbelievable! Thought there'd be security guards or something.'

'But it's only about six o'clock!'

Her heart thudded so loudly she wondered it didn't startle the baby.

*He's come. He's actually here. What on earth do I say? What is he doing here? At this hour! What if the nurse comes back?*

The silence stretched out. He just stood there,

looking at her, and the baby went on sucking, half-hidden by her T-shirt, and she looked down at him, and the bed, and glanced briefly up at Will. She could see how nervous he was, the way his hand twiddled round in his jeans pocket.

'What are you doing here, then?' Mia's voice came out wrong; she sounded cross.

'I don't know. I've been down on the beach.'

'All night?'

'Yes. I walked from Whitecross.'

'I thought I saw you last night, down in the car park.'

'No. Not me.'

'Well, I didn't think you would. I wasn't expecting you to or anything.'

'Don't say anything, Mia. I mean –'

'What?'

'I don't know.'

More silence.

'Can I see him?'

'In a minute. He's feeding still.'

'What's he look like?'

'Just a baby.'

*Will looks all wrong. In here, with his jeans and old coat and scruffy trainers.*

Her heart was beating too fast to think straight. He had come, then, he couldn't keep away after all. He looked so scared and ill at ease it gave her a sort of confidence; she handled the baby as if she was sure of how to do it, supported his head, put him against her shoulder so he could burp up the excess milk and air.

'So. Here he is.'

She wanted to say *our baby*, but she didn't.

Suddenly Will was crying.

It was a bit like seeing her dad cry. Awful. He tried to hide it; he went over to the window and looked out, but she saw.

'How did you find me?' she eventually asked his turned-away back.

'Becky. Yesterday. Came round after she saw you.'

Good old Becky. Dear, loyal friend.

'She said she'd never forgive me if I didn't come. Said no one would. After what you've been through.' Will's voice choked.

'So you didn't want to, then?' Mia's voice was cold.

'I didn't mean that.'

*We'll get into terrible trouble if they find him here*, Mia thought. And then, *So what?*

'I won't stay. Sorry.'

'Not sorry. Don't you want to see him close up? Now you're here?'

Will turned round, looked at her, then walked right over to the bed, sat down. She held the baby in the crook of her arm. Sleepy, milk-full, he rested there, eyes wide open.

Blue eyes. Like Will's.

Now her eyes filled with tears.

It wasn't supposed to be like this. This awkward, terrified, too-young little family. No one knowing how to be.

Will stretched out his hand and lightly touched the baby's hair. Dark, like Mia's.

He got up abruptly, rushed out of the room, leaving the door swinging slightly. The baby, startled by the sudden movement, trembled in Mia's arms. His lip quivered.

'It's all right, little Birdy,' she soothed him.

She looked out towards the open doorway, the empty corridor. There was the distant bang of swing doors flapping back.

Deep in her belly, Mia felt something new and totally unexpected. Something small and warm. A tiny nugget of hope.

Will's trainers had left damp, sandy footprints over the grey floor tiles. Next to the vase of white lilies on the windowsill lay a small oval pebble from the beach. When she picked it up, it was still warm from his hand.

## CHAPTER SIX

'That it, then? Got everything?' Dad paused at the doorway, bags in both hands, and looked back at the room.

'What about the flowers?' The nurse nodded towards the white lilies on the windowsill; they'd opened right up in the heated room, so that the stamens spilled out like tongues, dripping thick yellow pollen over the white sill. Their scent was too strong.

Mia shook her head. 'Nah. Can't carry them.' She had the pebble, though, tucked in her jeans pocket for safe keeping.

She followed Dad and the nurse down the corridor; she wasn't allowed to carry the baby till they got outside the hospital. Something to do with insurance. He was swaddled round in the shawl from Becky's mum, his fingers poking through the cobwebby wool. Mia had wrestled him into a white Babygro first thing, as soon as they said she could go home – him screaming the whole time, resisting, refusing to let her bend his arms into the sleeves. Now she understood the reason for the open little dresses the hospital provided. And then, just as she got him sorted, he'd done a huge poo – that tarry black stuff the nurse called meconium, which all newborn babies do at first – and it had squirted round the edges of the nappy and down the legs of the Babygro and she'd had to start all over again. Then she had to get herself washed and dressed, and that was a nightmare, too, the baby still screaming and upset, and she found she was leaking – milk from her painful, swollen breasts seeping out through her T-shirt, leaving two dark round patches that everyone would see. She didn't have anything else to wear, though.

'There you go, then.'

Mia carefully took the baby from the nurse's arms, cradled him in her own. That was it, then. She was free to go.

'Bye, then, Mia. Good luck! Don't forget, anything worrying you, just phone the community midwife's number. She'll be coming round to see you at home anyway. You've got the number? And the health visitor?'

Dad nodded. He patted his shirt pocket. 'All here. Thanks, then.'

The nurse was still watching from the steps as Mia followed slowly after her father, clutching the baby to her. What if she dropped him here, in the car park? She held him so tight he started to whimper. *Don't*, she hissed under her breath. *Don't cry now, please.* It seemed a million miles to the car.

While Dad stacked the bags in the back, Mia leaned against the passenger door. A light wind was blowing; it ruffled her hair. She held her face up, eyes closed, to feel the sun. Such a relief, to be outside, out of that stuffy hot room where someone was always watching, listening in, looking for your mistakes.

'Hop in the back, then. You'd better put the seat belt on, then hold him tight. I haven't got one of those baby seats for him yet. Haven't had a moment.'

'Dad! I told you. It's not safe. And it's illegal!'

'Yes, well, I'm sorry, Mia, but I've still been trying to work while all this has been going on. You can't take grandpaternity leave, you know. I'm doing my best.'

Mia closed her eyes again, blocked out the voice. She wished she could just walk home. Leave the baby in the car and start walking. Along the river, down to the estuary, then all the way along the beach to Whitecross. And further. Just keep on walking.

A little hand clawed through the shawl at her T-shirt. His head batted against her, searching her out. She felt the still-strange sensation of warmth flooding in her breasts, as if they were something quite separate from her. Her milk. *The let-down reflex.* All these things had a name, she was discovering. So weird. Her body knowing she was a mother, responding as it should, without her having any say in it.

What should she do now? Dad was concentrating on starting the engine. He glanced at her in the mirror briefly – 'Ready?' – and she nodded, and he started off. Once she was sure he couldn't see her, she pulled up her damp T-shirt and unwrapped the baby a bit, so he could find her nipple and start to suck. As long as they didn't see anyone they knew. Didn't brake suddenly. Didn't crash.

It was odd, driving into Whitecross along the main Ashton road, past the stone cross, the off-licence, the old garage. They went past the row of lime trees next to the bus stop. Her bus stop, where she'd spent so much time last summer, hanging out with Becky, and Will, and everyone. It all looked exactly the same. There was no one around this time of day; no one to witness her return, this new Mia, with a newborn baby cradled in her arms. The news would already have gone round the straggle of houses in the village – a brief ripple of gossip. *She's had it, then? A boy. How will they manage? That poor man. And him a teacher.* The shaken heads.

Arriving at the house was a different matter. She'd only been away a couple of days, but it felt so much longer. She'd crossed over to a new world, hadn't she? Where she was now *mother*. The house itself seemed smaller, messier, darker. Mia stood in the hall, the baby in her arms, and looked around her. Dad had made some sort of an effort: there were flowers from the garden in vases everywhere, even the kitchen.

She slumped down on the sitting-room sofa. Ginger-and-white cat hairs were stuck all over the cushions. He could have cleared them up! But he wouldn't have noticed, would he? It had never bothered her before. The baby trembled in her arms, his eyes all round and big and staring. At least he wasn't yelling any more, like when they'd first got out of the car.

'Shall I bring the Moses basket downstairs for you? You could lie him down in it for a while, give your arms a rest! We could put it near the French windows. That's what we did when you were a baby. You liked to watch the leaves in the ash tree.'

Mia didn't answer. She was so tired. Her legs ached just from that short walk at the hospital and then in from the drive. There was a lump in her throat.

Dad reappeared with the basket and put it down beside her.

'Now. Glass of juice or a Coke or something else? Hungry?'

She shook her head.

He kept talking from the kitchen, clunking mugs down on the table, filling the kettle.

'We can't keep calling him Baby, can we? Any ideas yet?'

It washed over her; the dreary, everyday ordinariness of home. She was back. This was it now. Her life, how it was going to be. Like a huge grey wave, swamping her.

Suddenly she was stricken with sobs which wouldn't stop. She was flooded with them, shuddering and heaving and sobbing her heart out.

*It's too much. I can't do this. I've made a terrible mistake.*

Dad came and sat down beside her. He put his arm round her shoulders and held her. She let him. It felt nice. She wanted to lean back into him and let him take over. She'd be a little child again, and he'd be the daddy, and he'd make everything all right.

'I know, I know,' he said softly, over and over. He didn't, though. How could he? He hadn't a clue what it was like. Not really. His face was furrowed with worry.

Once she'd got to the hiccuping stage, he relaxed a bit. 'Here, hand him over, and you put your feet up and get some sleep.' He arranged the cushions behind her. Patted her arm.

He moved on to the armchair near the window and lay the baby along his knees, so he could look straight up at him. 'Here you are, Baby. Little blue-eyed boy. Home now, Baby Blue.'

Mia watched them for a moment. Baby Blue. It was from a song Dad used to listen to, wasn't it?

She closed her eyes, let herself drift, let the sound of his voice soothe her, too.

Dad's words got through, though, as he chattered on to the baby. 'Do you like the flowers? All freshly picked this morning. Julie arranged them in the vases to welcome you home.'

*Julie. She was here, then. In the morning, which meant she must've stayed the night. So while I've been in hell in hospital, having a bloody baby, Dad has been sleeping with my old teacher. Great welcome. Some home.*

Mia curled herself round into a ball. Wished she were dead.

She was woken by the sound of the doorbell, and voices: Dad's and someone else's.

'Come on in,' he was saying. 'They're both asleep. No, it's fine.'

Her belly was full of the dizzy, sinking feeling that

had accompanied every waking up: *where's the baby?* She swung her legs round and sat up. He was tucked in the basket under the blanket, but he looked all wrong, she couldn't see his face. Dad had put him in face down. You were not supposed to do that any more. The baby could suffocate. They'd showed her in the hospital how to put him on his back, or his side. Mia grabbed at the basket and that startled him. His arms shot out, and his first muffled cries bleated into the room as Dad opened the sitting-room door, and behind him she saw the face of Will's mother, Annie. Oh no.

Mia held the wailing baby too tight. His face got redder, like hers, like Dad's. Annie came to the rescue.

'Oh, Mia, I'm so sorry. My ringing at the door. I've woken him up. Look, I'll come back later.'

'How about a cup of tea or something? I'll make us all one. Mia? Tea? Or juice or something?' Dad had picked up the cue.

*They are both so obvious*, Mia thought. *Trying to be understanding. Not to interfere. Annie has probably been reading up about it. Or talking to her friend who works with teenage mums.*

Meanwhile the baby screamed the house down, his little fists curled tight, his eyes squeezed shut, his body arching away from her. He'd probably stop crying immediately if Annie picked him up. Someone calm and sensible. A proper mother. But she wouldn't let her. No way.

Annie brought in a tray with a glass of apple juice, and an orange divided into easy-to-eat segments, and two digestive biscuits on a plate. She set it down on the side table.

'Shall I take him while you have a drink?' she offered, too thoughtfully.

Mia shook her head. 'I'll feed him first.' She didn't smile.

'OK. I'll pop back later, shall I? If you don't mind? I just wanted to meet him, you know, and see how you are, Mia. Is there anything you need?'

The question hung unanswered. So much she needed, and impossible to ask for any of it. Annie wanted something, too; Mia could tell that Annie was longing to hold the baby, to claim him: *my grandson, too.*

It seemed that was what all the grown-ups wanted. Their share. Apart from her own mother, of course. She'd made it quite clear that she would not be part of the childcare arrangements. And anyone might have thought Mia would be only too glad to hand the baby over, get a break for a few minutes. Yet something fierce and stubborn deep inside her resisted them, wanted to hang on tight, keep the baby close to her. *Hands off. Leave us alone.*

*Does she know that Will came to the hospital?* Mia thought she didn't. Will wouldn't have told anyone, especially not Annie. He knew she was already in too much of a panic about him messing up his exams.

'Poor Baby,' she whispered into his damp hair. His head still smelled of her body, the rich iron smell of blood. He was so new, and frail, and vulnerable. He needed her. She mustn't let him down now. 'Let's go upstairs, Birdy. Out of the way.'

She walked really carefully up the wooden stairs, supporting his head against her shoulder with one hand, the other around his bottom. That meant no spare hands to hold the rail, so she had to be especially careful. The kitchen door creaked open: Dad was watching her. She ignored him. Behind him, Annie was silhouetted against the window, mug of tea in one hand, watching, too. Neither said anything.

Mia kicked shut the bedroom door behind her and lay down with the baby on the single bed. Someone had put a vase of lilac on the dresser. The photograph frames had been rearranged, the one with her mother in it pushed further back. Mia saw all this in an instant; evidence of someone being here, in *her* room. It had better not have been *that woman*. Miss Julie Blackman. Her old teacher. Dad's girlfriend. Disgusting.

Mia fed the baby, propped up against the pillows

like she'd learned at the hospital. They'd been surprised she'd kept going this long, even. Expected her to give up after the first few tries, *like so many of you young girls,* but she'd been determined to give it a go. She'd read up about it, how important it was to try to breastfeed the new baby, in the old baby book her own mother must've used. The spine of the book was torn from being opened so much.

Mum was busy with her own life now, in Bristol. With Bryan. A baby didn't fit in with that new life. She hadn't wanted Mia to have him in the first place. She'd thought Mia was throwing her life away. It had nearly been the end of her, she'd told Mia back in the autumn, having three children. Nearly four. She'd had a miscarriage with the last one. Only now was she '*beginning to get my life back. At my age!*'

Through the window Mia watched the sunlight catching the top of the ash tree. No leaves yet; the black buds still tightly furled on the tips of the branches. Tiredness washed over her. She dozed with the baby still held against her breast. He dozed, too. His lip quivered as he slept. His hands were curled into tight little fists.

Mia heard Annie leave the house. She slept lightly then, still cradling the baby in her arms. She half woke, half dreamt. Names. She had to think of his name. They looped through her head like the continuous revolving adverts outside the supermarket in Ashton. *Ceri, meaning loved one; Kai, man of the sea; Leon, Leonardo, Luke*. She was getting closer. She'd know soon, what his name was.

The doorbell rang again. Dad's voice, registering surprise. Lots of voices, giggling, footsteps. The girls from school! She'd expected them at the hospital, but they'd not managed to get there before Dad collected her. They must have come straight here instead.

Mia eased the baby back down on to the bed and swung her legs over the edge. She felt stiff; her legs ached. She stood up, peered into the mirror on the chest of drawers, pulled her fingers through her hair to spike it up a bit, grimaced at herself. She smoothed the creases out of her T-shirt, pulled it down properly over her belly. No time to change. She picked the baby up again and padded carefully downstairs.

'Hello, everyone!'

Mia felt suddenly shy, the centre of attention. She sat down on the sofa with the baby. Becky, Tasha, Siobhan and Ali clustered round. To begin with they were quiet, reverent almost, drinking him in. The smallness of him. The aliveness. A real, live baby! Then everyone relaxed a bit.

'Oh, Mia, he's just so sweet! Look at his little

fingers. He's curling them round my thumb, look. He can grab things already!'

'Can I hold him?'

'No, I'm first. Mia said, when he wakes up a bit more.'

'His eyes are open. Look! Really blue. Not like yours, are they, Mia?'

Nudges. Smiles.

Mia laid the baby on Becky's lap. The others jostled in for a closer look.

'Give him a bit of space! You can each have a turn,' Becky said.

'Such tiny fingernails! Oh, Mia, he's adorable!'

'Go on, then. Open your presents!'

Ali pushed the pile of pretty packages closer to Mia. They'd been wrapped in different shades of blue tissue paper, tied up with silver ribbon. It must have taken them ages. Mia could imagine it: her friends all sitting round together at Becky's, after school. Laughing. Talking about her. Passing each other the tissue, the ribbon.

Mia unwrapped the parcels carefully, one by one, without tearing the paper. Ali twitched with impatience, exasperated at her for taking so long. Mia didn't know why she'd come round with the others. Curiosity? To gloat?

Inside, Mia was feeling strange. Even though the

presents were all for her, she felt left out of something.

'Thanks.'

There was a tiny silver mirror from Ali and a blue aromatherapy candle from Siobhan. Tasha gave her a turquoise beaded, embroidered purse and a small soft rabbit for the baby.

'Sweet,' Mia said. 'Thank you.' She stroked the rabbit's velvety ears.

Her hands rested limply in her lap amongst the sea of tissue. It had gone quiet. The girls were watching her, then each other. It wasn't going quite how they had imagined. They'd expected something more from her. More fun.

'Here, let me take him.' Tasha took the baby, so that Becky could give Mia the last present.

'It's a mobile thingy,' Becky explained. 'To hang in your room above his cot.'

Mia held up the silver stars. They revolved slowly, catching the light. It was beautiful. She listened to the whispering sounds the stars made as they touched each other in the draught. Everyone watched Mia, suddenly unsure.

Siobhan rallied. 'So, what was it like? Give us all the gruesome details!'

'Yuck! No thanks.' Ali screwed up her nose.

'Mum says, if women could know in advance what it was really like, then *nobody* but *nobody* would ever have a baby and the human race would all die out!'

'They'd do it some other way. Genetics. Cloning or something.'

'Those rich bitches all have Caesareans. *Too posh to push!*'

'But then you get a scar.'

'It's quite neat, though. Billie had one. Only because she had to, though. Emergency,' Tasha said.

'Who's Billie?'

'Tasha's half-sister.'

'So, Mia? Go on. Tell us.' Tasha smiled.

Dad opened the door. They all looked up guiltily, as if he'd caught them out.

'All right, girls? Don't wear her out. She's only just come home, remember.'

Ali spoke first. Of course. 'We just couldn't wait any longer, Mr Kitson – I mean *David*. Just *had* to see him.'

Mia scowled at Ali. Still at it, then. Flirting with Dad.

Siobhan put out her arms to take the baby from Tasha. 'My turn. I know how to do it. You have to hold the head up. Whoops.'

Mia winced. They were passing him round as if it were a party game.

Dad looked round the room. 'What's all this, then?

Presents? That's nice. Can one of you help clear up the paper?'

'We'll tidy up before we go.'

'Thanks, Becky. Everything OK? What's up with Baby Blue?'

'He doesn't like Ali. She's made him cry,' Siobhan teased.

'Shut up, you!'

'I'll take him again, shall I?' Becky said. The baby started to wail. 'Or maybe he's hungry. Mia?'

Mia had had enough. 'It's OK, Becks. Give him here. Careful.' *He's not a bloody parcel.*

She lifted up her T-shirt and the baby turned hungrily towards her. She bent forwards over him. *That smell. Sweet, milky baby smell.* She closed her eyes, shut them all out.

'Oh, my God! Look at you. Bloody hell, Mia. They're HUGE!'

'Shut up, Ali!' Tasha snapped back. 'Don't be so mean.'

Ali pouted and sulked. Becky and Siobhan smirked behind her back.

The baby wouldn't feed. She couldn't do it with everyone there, watching. Must have been mad to even think of it. They thought she was gross, the way she looked. The baby cried like a cat. His face had gone red and spotty. She wanted to cry, too.

Tasha came over and sat down next to Mia. She stroked the baby's head gently. Mia fought back the tears.

'He's really special, Mia. You're amazing. Coping with all this. Honestly. I know we don't have a clue, really.'

Mia looked gratefully at Tasha. She understood more than the others. Tasha was from a huge family: four proper brothers and sisters, and then an assortment of others, stepbrothers and stepsisters, and she was somewhere in the middle. So she was already an auntie at fifteen, several times over. If you went round her house, there were always small children and babies hanging out there. That's why they usually went to Becky's, instead. Or Mia's, where no one interfered. Well, used not to.

'What are they talking about?' Mia nodded her head towards the other girls, who were still giggling.

Tasha smoothed one finger along the baby's cheek. 'Ali's sixteenth, remember? She's having a party. Saturday week. Her parents are going out specially. Everyone will be there. We're getting really tarted up for it. Just for a laugh. Going shopping after school on Thursday.'

Mia curved her hand lightly round the baby's soft skull. If you looked closely, you could see the place where the bones hadn't yet fused together. *The fontanelle*. You could see it pulsing, like a heartbeat, through the membrane. *That's why you must be careful with a new baby's head*, she thought. And then, *So they are all going to a party. Except me.*

'I don't suppose you –' Tasha started, but Mia interrupted angrily.

'No. Of course I can't.'

Dad opened the door a second time and stood there, surveying the scene. He liked it when all the girls were here. He'd said so often enough. Today, though, for once, he was thinking about her. 'Time's up. End of visiting. Mia and the baby need a rest from you lot!' He smiled broadly at them. 'Come again another day, yes?'

Ali brushed against his arm when she left, on purpose. 'See you soon, then.' She said it to Mia, but it was Dad, *David*, she was smiling at.

Becky bundled the tissue paper into the kitchen bin on her way out. Tasha was the last to leave.

'I'd love to help, babysitting and that, when he's a bit bigger. When you're ready. Honestly.'

'Thanks, Tash.'

'Look, we'll come round after we've been shopping and show you what we've got. So you don't feel so left out. OK?'

The door slammed. Mia imagined them all going down the garden path, then up the lane to Becky's.

Talking about her. Feeling sorry for her. Planning what they'd wear for the party.

Everyone would be there.

Including Will.

Everyone except her. She was stuck here, now. Forever and ever.

## CHAPTER SEVEN

*D*awn. Mia sat on her bed with the curtains open, watching the sun rise while the baby sucked. He was putting on weight, like he was supposed to. Mia felt an inordinate and surprising pleasure that it was purely due to her that he was thriving. The health visitor had weighed him yesterday and written it down in a little red book. There was a graph you could fill in, plotting the gains in weight so you knew your baby was growing. It seemed, at last, that this was something at which she could succeed.

On a good day, that was. There were the other days, dark and depressing, when she couldn't even seem to find time to get dressed, and the baby grizzled, or bawled his head off, and she was totally alone with him for long, long hours while everyone else was at school.

The whole sky had turned from pink to a thin pale blue. The leaves on the ash tree outside Mia's bedroom window were beginning to open out now, fresh and green. Right at the top a blackbird was singing. Even from here, she could see its tiny throat reverberating as it sang its heart out.

When the baby cried, he opened his mouth so wide it became a red gaping hole. Mia would like to be able to open her mouth like that, to really let rip. The sound that would come out: what would it be? Rage? Grief? Hard to give something so raw a name. It was like there was a big bottomless pit inside her that nothing could fill up. She wanted. She needed. What?

Was it Will she was missing? The baby's birth had brought all that back again. She knew they weren't together any more; hadn't been, for months. But seeing him in the hospital, seeing his echo in the baby every hour of every day, it had all come flooding back. How she'd first felt about him.

She thought about what it would be like, him with her, sharing the baby together. His arms around her.

The baby was so little, and he needed so much, and she had to give it to him because she was all he had. Dad did his best, but there was so much he couldn't do. He had to go to work, for one thing. And he still had loads of work to do in the evenings, even when she most needed someone to give her a break. And no one could feed the baby but her. And that was what he needed; so often. She had had no idea. It was quite normal, the health visitor, Vicky, said. She was doing it perfectly, feeding him when he wanted, every couple of hours and sometimes more often.

'It's a full-time job, Mia,' she'd said yesterday, 'looking after a new baby. And you have to rest as much as you can. Eat well. Drink lots of water. Otherwise you'll be too exhausted to cope. Seriously. But it won't always be like this.' She'd smiled.

*Won't it?* Mia looked down at the baby. He'd stopped sucking and now turned his head to look up at her. His dark hair was damp and ruffled; his blue eyes tried to focus on her face. Will's eyes.

It was Thursday. Becky and Tasha and everyone might call round on their way back from shopping in Ashton after school. But that wouldn't be till about six, at the earliest. More than twelve hours away. Dad had got school and then a meeting. Vicky would probably call in the morning sometime. And the rest of the day it would be just the two of them, her and Baby. Perhaps, if it stayed sunny, she might take him out for the very first time.

They dozed together in the early-morning light. She was vaguely aware of the sounds of Dad getting up: water gushing in the bathroom, his feet along the landing and down the stairs, the radio on in the kitchen. The smell of burnt toast drifted upstairs. Just before he left, he tapped at her bedroom door.

'Mia? Awake yet? I've brought you a glass of orange.'

She woke up just enough to tug her T-shirt down over her breasts before Dad came in.

'Lovely morning. Sleep any better? How's my blue-eyed boy?'

Mia groaned. 'Don't wake him up, Dad.'

'How was the night?'

'I had to feed him about a million times.'

'You poor old thing. Still, he's only very little. He doesn't know about night and day yet, does he? He'll get the hang of it. I'm off now. You going to be all right? Becky's mum said she might call in on you later, OK? She'll bring you some lunch, knowing her. And you can phone me at school if you need to, for any reason.'

'Like what?'

'Oh, I don't know, Mia. But if there was an emergency or something. And there's Annie not far away, and the health visitor's coming, isn't she?'

'Stop fussing, Dad.'

'See you later, then. I'll try not to be too late home.' He leaned over and kissed the baby's head, and then hers.

She heard the front door slam, the car engine start up, the car crunching over gravel and then receding into the distance.

Mia thought about Will. When was the last time he'd kissed her? Months ago. Before she'd told him she was pregnant.

Will would be on his way to school now. If she went outside she might even see him walking down the lane to the bus stop. School was all revision classes, Becky said. Study leave started in a week or so, and then the first GCSE exams. At least she didn't have to do them.

Her body ached still. She longed to sleep and sleep, with no interruptions, for days, weeks. For a hundred years. *Like Sleeping Beauty*, Mia thought. *To be woken by a kiss from a handsome prince. As if.*

The doorbell rang. Mia woke with a start. The clock on the chest of drawers said eleven. She slid out of the covers so as not to disturb the baby, but too late; he woke abruptly and started to yell. The doorbell rang again. Must be Vicky. Mia pulled a fleece top over her T-shirt and then scrabbled around for the trousers she'd left in a heap on the floor. She snatched up the baby and padded downstairs.

'Sorry, Mia. Were you sleeping?'

Vicky smiled from the doorstep. She was quite young and had this broad, open face that instantly won you over. Fair, short hair, all messed up from where she ran her hands through it. There was nothing threatening or judgemental about her. So completely different from those nurses in hospital.

Vicky followed Mia into the sitting room. 'Shall I make us a drink? I'll take him, if you want to finish getting dressed. I know how hard it is, doing everything with one hand!'

Mia handed over the wailing baby. Vicky didn't jiggle him, like most people did with crying babies; she sat down quietly with him, cradled him, looked right into his screwed-up little face and talked gently, soothing him with words and closeness.

'It's hard, little one, isn't it? But you're OK. You keep telling us what it's like, that's right. You're safe here, sweetie. I'll hold you close and Mia will be back in a minute to feed you. She won't be long.'

Mia hovered in the doorway, listening to her words. She loved the way Vicky was with him; so quiet and gentle. The way she talked to him as if he understood everything. Then she turned and ran upstairs to get properly dressed. She combed her hair, glanced at her pale face in the mirror, stuck out her tongue at it.

She could still hear Vicky's voice, chatting to the baby. Finally, Mia went back downstairs and into the sitting room.

Vicky came in with her coffee and a glass of water for Mia. 'It's good to start going out and about again.

How about coming to the Young Parents' group I told you about? Wednesday mornings, in Ashton. There's a bus you can get into Ashton, isn't there?'

'I'll think about it.'

'There's a new girl, your sort of age. With a baby boy, too. She could do with some friends. She doesn't know anyone round here. She was with the fair, you know – travellers – but she's been poorly. Had to stay on behind.' Vicky turned her attention back to the baby. 'He's looking fantastic. Aren't you so clever! We won't weigh him today. We don't want him upset all over again.'

Already, Vicky had become a sort of friend. She understood what it was like. She had a child of her own, although she was so young. 'It was because of having him, at seventeen,' she'd told Mia the first time she'd come to the house, 'that I worked out what I wanted to be.'

'And how are *you* feeling today, Mia?' Vicky asked her, once the baby was settled.

'Tired. But all right. It is getting better, I think.'

'Good. Early days still, anyway. Take it easy, yes? But you don't want to be on your own all the time. Any of your friends coming round today?'

'Maybe, later,' Mia said. 'They're going shopping after school.'

'Must be nearly exam time?'

'Yes. Next week, I think. Or the one after – I lose track.'

'What will you do, do you think?'

Mia shook her head.

'When you were still at school, what did you want to do?'

'Nothing, really. That was the trouble. I don't want to go to college or anything. Not like my sisters. So I'm a big disappointment, I guess. Useless at everything.'

Vicky frowned. 'No, you're not. Not at this, you're not.' She nodded her head at the calm, contented baby.

'This doesn't count. This is just one more mistake.'

'Don't say that! You don't mean that! Your dad loves the baby. It's obvious.'

'Maybe. But it's not what he wanted me to do, is it?'

'Don't start thinking like that, Mia. Concentrate on how well you're doing now. You're a really good mother. I should know. I get to see all sorts, I can tell you. Being *young* doesn't mean you can't do it well. *And* enjoy it. You've got a happy, healthy baby.' She started to gather up her things. 'I've got to get on now. I'm seeing Colleen next, in Ashton. The girl I told you about. I'll tell her you might be there next Wednesday, shall I?'

Mia shrugged. 'Dunno. Maybe.' Talking about school had made her grumpy again.

'Please. Try?'

'OK.'

She stood on the front doorstep to watch Vicky drive off. The sun had moved round; it was shining through the tree, casting bright patterns on the grass. The bluebells in the long grass under the wall had opened out, a deep blue mist. She'd take the baby out into the garden later. *The baby*. She couldn't keep thinking of him like that. He needed his name. She'd decide today.

She was still standing there when Becky's mum turned up, a dish under one arm covered with a tea towel.

'Such a lovely day, I walked!' she called out to Mia. 'You enjoying the sun, Mia?'

'The health visitor just left.' Mia frowned. She didn't feel like seeing anyone else right now. Having to talk.

'Oh, right. Good. Everything all right? Did your dad say I'd call?'

Mia nodded.

'I've brought you some lunch. Vegetarian lasagne. You can keep it for supper if you've already eaten.'

Mia didn't reply.

'I'll put it in the fridge for you.'

'It's OK. I'll take it.'

'No, you stay in the sun a bit longer. You look a bit peaky. How is Baby?'

Mia knew she was dying to see him. 'He's fine,' she said. 'Sleeping.'

'Can I just have a tiny peep? I won't wake him. And I'll put this in the kitchen for you.'

Becky's mum went inside; reluctantly Mia followed. From the sitting-room doorway she watched her peer into the wicker basket, disappointed not to be able to hold him.

Becky's mum smiled at her. 'How are you, love? Eating well, I hope. None of that dieting nonsense while you're breastfeeding, eh? I remember it well. Always hungry. Not that I ever stopped eating for two.' She laughed, and patted her round stomach, and Mia allowed herself a small smile back.

She was glad the room was tidy. And that she was up and dressed. Everything looked as if it was under control. No room for any gossip. Becky's mum wouldn't be nasty about it, but sometimes she just couldn't stop herself talking. Telling everyone. A bit like Becky. Although Becky had been really brilliant about not telling anyone when Mia was first pregnant. A real friend.

'Now, do you need any shopping? Got enough fruit and bread and milk?'

Mia nodded. *Why didn't she just go?*

'Oh! Look. He's waking up!' Becky's mum leaned over the wicker basket, grinning and clucking. 'What a little sweetie. Oh, he's just the best! Such a tiny little love!' She turned back towards Mia. 'Can I pick him up?'

'OK.'

At least she'd asked. Mia noticed how confidently Becky's mum scooped up the baby, wrapped him in the blanket, held him cupped against her shoulder. He looked safe there. She couldn't help comparing what it had been like seeing her own mother hold him, back in the hospital. How clumsy and uneasy Mum had been, how quickly she'd handed him back.

Becky's mum loved babies. Becky had told her often enough. Why not make the most of it?

Mia looked longingly at the sunny garden. Just a few minutes wouldn't hurt. He'd been fed. Wasn't crying.

Becky's mum smiled at Mia. 'Do you want a few minutes' break from him? I'll keep him happy while you have a bath or read a book or something. If you want.'

'I need some air,' Mia said. 'I'll just go down the lane for a bit. He'll be all right, won't he?'

A big grin spread across Becky's mum's face. 'Of course. Don't you worry. Go on, then, love. We'll be fine, won't we, little chap? And it's a real treat for me!' She patted the baby's back gently, talked to him in baby talk. He seemed to like it.

*Just for a little while, then.* Mia kissed him goodbye.

The sunlight was so bright she had to screw up her eyes. It felt amazing, to walk away from the house and down the lane. Empty-handed. She'd head for the sea, of course.

The tide was out. It felt cooler here. A wind off the sea blew her hair back from her face. She tipped her face up, to feel the air and the sun; closed her eyes. The mew of gulls, the thin piping of oystercatchers, wind rustling dry grass. The suck and swallow of the waves dragging pebbles. She felt a huge weight drop away. She was still her. Mia.

She walked along the beach a little way, hunting out a flat boulder that had dried in the sun, just the right size for sitting on. She felt strangely light and empty. Her arms – free, nothing to hold. She scooped up a handful of gravelly sand, let it trickle through her fingers.

He'd be all right. It was only for a few minutes. Just to draw breath.

The list of names. She'd almost decided. Ceri or Kai. She'd know. It would come to her if she waited.

Sunlight flickered on the water. It was warm on her back, though her face was still cool. She moved her head, felt how stiff and tight the muscles were in her neck, her shoulders. She took a deep breath. And another. Closed her eyes. Inside her head she saw a silver bird, wings stretched out, soar in a clear blue sky. There was a sound too, like a seabird's call. *Kai*, it called. *Kai*.

She woke from her daydream with a jolt. How long had she been there? A real voice was calling her name. She squinted her eyes against the light; the dark shape of a figure was stumbling along the foreshore towards her. Wind whipped his hair. It was him. She knew it instantly. She steeled herself for the meeting, but her heart thudded and her armpits prickled with sweat. How would he be? She'd not seen anything of him since that moment in the hospital. His abrupt departure.

'Will! What are you doing here?'

'Bunked off, didn't I?'

*Will, golden boy, predicted A grades in all ten GCSEs, bunking off school?*

'Thought it was you. But I couldn't quite believe – you know. That you'd be out,' he said.

'Makes it sound like I've been in prison or something.' She had, sort of.

'Where's the – ?'

'Baby?'

'Yes.'

He couldn't look at her directly; stood half-turned away, hands in his pockets, staring at the water.

'Becky's mum's with him.'

'Is he all right?'

'What's it to you?'

She saw her words sting him. She'd meant to hurt. Why should he get away with it? He was the baby's father and yet here he was, walking along the beach, doing exactly what he wanted. Nothing had changed for him. He'd done nothing to help her, nothing to make it any easier. All he'd thought about was himself. Even coming to the hospital like that, he'd only done that because of what Becky had said. Had just turned and left her there. Hadn't even said goodbye.

He'd never have thought anything about it ever again, after she found she was pregnant last autumn. Let her get rid of it without another thought. She could still remember his words, when she said about the abortion. *It's not so terrible, is it?* And then, after he heard that she'd walked out of the hospital, his complete horror that there would be a baby after all. He'd just avoided her. Mia had seen more of his mother, Annie, than she had of him.

But he hadn't been seeing anyone else, Becky told

her. And Mia had hoped – well, she should have known better than to hope, shouldn't she?

Will picked up a handful of small pebbles and chucked them in the shallow water. They made a sound like gunshot.

Her anger died down again, coiled back to a small tight knot deep inside her. Too late, though. His mood had already turned cold: hands in pockets, staring out across the water as if there was something more interesting there than empty water, clouds, sky.

'Sorry I said that.' She said it through gritted teeth. 'Will?'

His shoulders hunched.

'It's the truth,' he said coldly. 'It isn't anything to do with me.'

His turned-away back infuriated her. He wouldn't even face her. How cowardly was that?

'I don't think so.' Mia's voice was tight with fury now. 'I think there's a different truth, actually. Whether you want to hear it or not. The baby's everything to do with you, that's the real truth, isn't it?'

There. It was out now. She'd said it. She'd blown it totally. So what? Better to speak out than keep it all pent up inside her. It was the truth.

He walked along the shore a little further, picked

up another handful of pebbles, chucked them in. Kept his back to her.

Mia was on a roll now.

'This is the first time I've been out,' she said, 'in over a week.'

Silence.

'I've hardly had more than two hours' sleep at a stretch.'

No answer.

'That's a kind of torture, isn't it? Sleep deprivation. You'd know about that, wouldn't you? I expect your mother writes letters about it to Amnesty International.'

Still he didn't speak.

'While you've been bunking off school and walking on the beach every morning for a week.'

She'd like to spit in his face, to shake his rigid, sulking body, force him to look at her, to see what was happening to her, to look her in the eyes. But just the thought of touching him turned her to jelly. Even though she was so angry she could hardly speak, she still longed for him to turn round, touch her, put his arms round her.

She'd have forgiven him everything. If it hadn't been for Becky's mum waiting for her at home, she'd even have asked him to come back with her. What kind of a mug did that make her? *Doormat*, Becky would say. *Let him walk all over you.*

But then it was easy enough to think that when it couldn't happen.

Because if Becky's mum hadn't been there, she'd have had the baby with her now.

And that's how it would always be now. Her-and-the-baby.

Will's back was still turned away. Mia moved forwards, caught his arm, saw his flushed face. She'd make him think about it. What it meant. Her baby, who was also his, whether he liked it or not.

He pulled his arm away from her.

'I'm going to call him Kai. It means "man of the sea",' Mia blurted out.

She could see sweat break out on his forehead. His fair hair was damp already from the sea spray.

'So, what do you think?'

'I've never heard of the name before,' Will mumbled. 'It doesn't matter.'

'Yes, it does. Names do matter.'

'You know what I mean.'

'You don't like the name, do you?'

'It doesn't matter what I think.' He chucked another handful of stones into the sea. His face was closed to her, a mask.

*There was no point in any of this*, Mia thought. She had made everything worse. She turned away. 'Got to get back.'

A white seabird drifting on the air currents above the bay whimpered and mewed like a baby. Her breasts felt tight. She'd start leaking soon.

She crunched back up the beach; wouldn't allow herself to look back. *Don't think about him now. Leave him be. Keep hold of being angry with him. It's easier that way.*

She kicked at an empty Coke can and the sound of it banging into rock gave her a second of pleasure. What she'd really like to do was scream. Scream and scream till there was no breath left in her lungs.

Mia started to run as soon as she reached the lane. It was as if a thread was pulling her, winding her back in. The strangest feeling, deep in her body. She even imagined she heard the baby's cry, long before it could be possible. Her T-shirt had two dark patches from leaking milk.

She flew through the gate. The front door was open on to the garden and Becky's mum was standing in the doorway with the baby at her shoulder, patting his back and cooing and jiggling him, as he hiccuped his way through sobs. Mia found herself crying, too.

She should never have left him. He'd no way of knowing she was ever coming back. He sobbed as if she'd gone forever.

'He's only just started crying, Mia. He was fine until just now! I expect he's hungry.'

Mia wrenched off her sandy boots and then gathered the bundle into her arms.

Becky's mum hovered anxiously. 'The lasagne's heating up in the oven. Ten more minutes and it'll be ready. OK? Will you be all right, Mia? I'm sorry but I've got to get on now. I'm already late for work.'

'Sorry. He's just hungry. I shouldn't have left him so long. I didn't mean to.' She looked up. Becky's mum was still hovering, as if waiting for her to say something more. 'Thank you for looking after him. Tell Becks to come round later.'

'All right, love. Have a good afternoon. You'll be all right? Sure?'

Mia nodded. Why couldn't she just go away now? She needed to cry and cry. About leaving Kai. About Will. About the whole bloody mess.

Becky's mum left.

'I'm so sorry. Sorry, sorry, sorry for leaving you.' She nuzzled her face into the baby's and his little tongue licked her nose. Her tears made his head damp. 'But I found your name. I had to be away from you to think of it. You're Kai. That's who you are.'

She whispered the name into his ear over and over, as if it was a magic spell.

'Kai'. One letter away from 'Mia'. Close, but completely different. He could be whoever he was with a name like that.

The afternoon dragged by. Kai was unsettled. He grizzled and whimpered as soon as she went any distance from him. He needed to be held close, and fed, almost all the time. That was her fault, she knew, for leaving him like that. She wouldn't do it again.

Mia kept watching the clock, listening out for the sound of voices and laughter coming up the path. She turned the television on, but the programmes jarred her nerves: ridiculous quiz shows, children's cartoons. The jangling music made Kai's limbs jerk as he dozed on her lap on the sofa.

The doorbell rang, finally, at six fifteen. Becky stood on the doorstep, smiling.

'Where's everyone else?'

'Sorry, Mia. They've gone straight home. It's just me.'

Typical. Couldn't they make the slightest effort? Didn't they understand how much it mattered to her? Especially Tasha.

She tried not to let her disappointment show too

much. Faithful Becky was already in the kitchen, putting on the kettle, chatting about the day and the shopping.

'So we ended up buying identical skirts! Well, except Ali. Then we went in Jigsaw, just to look, and they've got these absolutely beautiful tops, lined in silk. Ninety-six quid, can you believe it? For a top!'

'I've decided on his name.'

'You what?'

'The baby's name. Kai.'

Becky squealed. 'Oh, it's lovely.'

She leaned over the baby. 'Hello, Kai. It's perfect for him. I love it. It's very unusual. Special. What does your dad think about it?'

'He doesn't know yet.'

'Well, he'll like it, won't he?'

'I saw Will, Becks.'

'Where? He never came round?'

'No, no – on the beach. Your mum looked after Kai for me and there he was. I didn't expect him to be there.'

'He's not been in school all week. Is he ill?'

'No. Bunking off. Must be catching.'

Becky giggled. 'So? What did he say? Come on, tell me! Everything.'

'I told him about Kai's name. He doesn't like it.'

'Well – who cares? We love it, don't we, Kai? What else?'

'Nothing. We didn't talk about anything. It was horrible. I got cross.'

Becky sighed. 'Oh, Mia, you're hopeless! And you still like him, don't you?'

'Yes. But it's no good. He doesn't want anything to do with me. Or *him*.' Mia kissed the top of Kai's head.

'He's really stressed, Mia. Exams. Parents. You know what they're like.'

He *was stressed? Why did everyone think about it from his point of view? Even Becky! It was so unfair.*

'Forget about all that now, anyway. Let's get some supper together.' Becky started opening cupboards, looking in the fridge. 'Blimey! It's stacked full of stuff!'

'Everyone keeps bringing meals round. All the mothers,' Mia said. 'Let's have the rest of the lasagne. Your mum's. You make a salad.'

*Becky should be the one with the baby, not me*, Mia thought. She was so sensible, so practical. She'd already come up with the brilliant idea of putting Kai in the baby sling to keep him quiet. He wouldn't be put down in his basket this evening. Cried every time they tried.

The baby sling had been a present from Annie. It

meant Mia could walk around with him strapped to her front and still have both hands free. Only his head was so wobbly, it kept slipping sideways. Perhaps he was still too small for it.

'What time's your dad back?'

'Any time now.'

'I've got to go in a minute. French oral next week, then English Paper One.' Becky pulled a face. 'Got to do revision every night except Saturday. I promised.'

'Come round Sunday first thing, won't you? I want to hear all about Ali's party. Everything. Promise?'

'You might not want to know.'

'What do you mean by that?'

'Nothing. OK. I promise. All the gory details. If you insist.' She hugged Mia goodbye. 'You going to be all right?'

'Yes. Dad'll be back soon. Go on, off you go. See you Sunday.'

## CHAPTER EIGHT

'Where are you off to?'

'Out.'

'I can see that. But where?'

'What is this, Dad? I don't have to tell you where I'm going all the time!'

'But your mother will be here any moment. She's driving all the way from Bristol to see you and Kai. You can't just disappear for the day.'

'I'm only going for a walk.'

'Well, how long for?'

'I dunno. Not long. I've just got to get out of this place. It's doing my head in.'

'You shouldn't be taking him out in this wind, anyway. He's not wrapped up enough.'

'Shut up, Dad. Stop telling me what to do.'

'Well, you've got to think about him, you know, not just yourself all the time. He's only a week old.'

'Thirteen days, actually.'

'Very little. At least put a hat on him.'

'He's tucked under my jacket. Warm. OK?'

Mia slammed the door behind her. *Nag nag nag.* He didn't give up. She would go crazy if she stayed living here. She'd have to work out something else. Soon.

Once she'd got out of the garden and on to the lane, she fished a little turquoise cotton hat from her pocket and put it on Kai's head. She wasn't going to let Dad see her do it. He'd think she was doing it because he'd said to. Didn't give her credit for having any sense. Kai twisted his face at the unfamiliar feeling of the hat and she stroked her finger along his cheek. *Don't cry. Not now. Please.*

Instead of down the hill to the sea, she went up the lane towards Becky's house. Stupid idea, she realized as soon as she reached the house and saw Becky's curtains still drawn. She'd forgotten how early it was for a Sunday morning. She'd been up with Kai since six. It must only be about ten.

Becky's mum waved from the kitchen window and came to the front door to let her in.

'Lovely to see you two! That's a good way of carrying him. Asleep? Come on in, love. Becky's still in bed, I'm afraid.'

Mia hesitated.

'I'll make you a drink and you can go up and see if she's awake. Bit of a late night. Ali's party.'

'Yes. I know.'

Mia walked carefully upstairs, still in her coat, with Kai in the baby sling. She opened Becky's door a slit and peeped in.

Becky opened her eyes and groaned. 'Mum?'

'No, it's me, Mia. Are you awake?'

'Just. What are you doing here?'

'Came to see you. Find out about last night.'

'What time is it?'

'Dunno. I've been up hours.'

'My mouth feels terrible. Come in properly. And shut the door.'

Mia sat on the bottom of the bed. Kai stayed asleep.

'He's wearing a hat. Sweet.'

'So? How was it?'

'Give me a moment to wake up, Mia.'

Mia went over to the window and opened the curtains. Becky groaned as the sunlight flooded into the room.

'Sorry. I'll just open them a bit.'

'It's too bright. My head aches something rotten.'

The bedroom door opened.

'Here you are!' Becky's mum brought in two glasses of orange juice and put them on the bedside table. She smiled at them and then went back out.

'Your mum's amazing!' Mia said. 'She waits on you hand and foot, doesn't she?'

'She likes doing it. She'd do it for you if you let her. She says you can leave Kai with her any time, when she's not working. She loves babies.'

Mia pulled a face. 'My mother's coming today from Bristol. A miracle.'

'*Alice*,' Becky said.

They both giggled at the way Mia's mother insisted on Mia using her name.

'Will *Julie* be visiting, too?'

'She hasn't been round all week. Perhaps she and Dad have had a row.'

'More likely she's just giving you some space. With the new baby and that.'

'Maybe. I don't want to see her.'

'What does your mum think about it?'

'How should I know? Nothing, probably. It's none of her business any more. She's got Bryan, hasn't she?'

'Yes, but that doesn't stop people still *feeling* something, does it? About their ex?'

Mia shrugged.

'So, is this Bryan coming as well?'

'Hope not. Bad enough having Mum. I mean *Alice*. Now, tell me about last night. What happened?'

'We-ell,' Becky dragged out the word, playing for time. 'Everyone was there. The whole tutor group, practically. All the boys got completely pissed. Most of the girls, too. Rob puked all over the kitchen floor. Siobhan got off with Liam.'

'No!'

'After all that saying she didn't fancy him. I know!'

'What about you?'

'Nothing. Well, I had a really good laugh, and danced a lot. Drank too much. Nothing else. As usual.' She pulled a face.

'Ah. Poor you. So, no luck with Matt?'

'He's not interested, Mia. It's obvious. We have a good laugh and that, but nothing more.'

'And Will?'

'What about him?'

'For heaven's sake, Becky, stop spinning it out. Just tell me!'

'He was ratted. I've never seen him so pissed.'

'And?'

'He didn't know what he was doing.'

'What, though?'

'It didn't mean anything, Mia. Stop asking me. It isn't fair.'

'Well, you have to tell me now. It was Ali, wasn't it?'

'Yes.'

'I'll kill her.'

'He was drunk, Mia. It doesn't mean anything.'

'What were they doing?'

'I don't know. I wasn't watching. Trying not to.'

'Kissing?'

'Yes. I don't know.'

'Did they sleep together?'

'Of course not – least, well, I don't know, do I? Don't do this, Mia. It's pointless. You're just getting yourself into a state.'

'That's it. I'll kill him. While I'm stuck at home, can't even go to the party, he's getting off with Ali. He knew I'd find out.'

'Well, she's been after him for months. It's surprising it's taken this long if you think about it. He's done quite well to resist. She's pretty determined, our Ali.'

'Not *our* Ali. Whose side are you on?'

'Yours of course, but you've got to understand something, Mia! Listen!'

'I hate her. To think she was in my house only days ago! Holding my baby. Mine and his. How could she?'

'Mia, you've got to get a grip. You've got to stop thinking about Will like that. It's too hard on everyone. He's a sixteen-year-old bloke, Mia!'

'You're the one who told me that a baby needs both parents. You did. I distinctly remember.'

'I know. I still do think that. But it won't happen

overnight, will it? You have to be patient and give him some time.'

'What about me? All you can think about is *him* having time. What about *me* having time? I'm the one who's up all night, and holding him all day, and I can't even come up here without having him tied round my neck. I thought you were my friend.'

'You're making my headache worse. I don't want to argue with you, Mia.'

'You shouldn't have told me, then.'

'You asked. You went on and on about it. I told you it wasn't fair.'

Mia got up off the bed. The sudden movement jolted the baby, who started to whimper. 'Shut up!' she hissed. 'Don't you start now. I can't stand it.'

'Mia! Hang on. Don't go!'

But Mia was already out of the door and halfway down the stairs. The kitchen door opened as she went past.

'You're not going already? I thought you and Beck –'

Becky's mum's voice trailed after Mia as she opened the front door and rushed out. At the gate, she turned back briefly and caught a glimpse of Becky's face pressed to the window upstairs. Her best friend. Saying all that horrible stuff. Even if she was right. Which she wasn't, of course. How unfair could you get? Mia bit her lip hard to stop the tears.

Will. How could he? And with Ali? The thought of him kissing Ali like he used to kiss her, stroking her hair: it was unbearable.

Where could she go? Not home, not now, after this. She imagined the day ahead. Mum would be arriving at the house. They'd all have Sunday lunch. Afterwards, Dad would suggest a stroll down to the sea, or across the fields. Back for afternoon tea. Pleases and thank-yous and everyone pretending that they were a normal happy family. They would look like it, from the outside: father, mother, daughter, grandson. Except that nothing was what it appeared to be: her parents no longer loving one another, both wishing they were with someone else; and her, Mia, the bad, ungrateful daughter, with the baby no one had wanted.

No one but her, that is. Eventually.

Such a thin thread, holding on to his life. So easily he might not have been.

Mia turned up the lane and kept walking, fast, not really caring that what she was doing would make everything worse. She took the turning towards Will's house. What if Ali was there? Had been all night? Surely not. She didn't think Will would dare do that, not after everything that had happened. And it was

Ali's party – she couldn't have just left everyone to it, could she? Even if her parents hadn't been coming back till really late. More likely he'd come home from the party and crashed out. Was still sleeping. Not for much longer, though. Just wait till she set eyes on him. She could feel the anger burning up through her body. Even her fingertips quivered with it. She wanted to smash things up. Scream and hit and bite and kick. Tell him exactly what she thought.

Annie, Will's mother, must have seen her coming up the lane. She was already at the front garden gate as Mia arrived. Not exactly barring the way, although Mia wasn't sure. Annie's face was tight, serious. She took off her gardening gloves and put down the fork she'd been using.

'Mia.'

Kai began to whimper again.

'You're using my sling. Well done! It's so much easier like that, isn't it? You can do proper walks, not like with a pram or a buggy.' Annie's voice sounded falsely bright. 'So, where are you two off to?'

It was obvious, wasn't it?

'See Will.' Mia mumbled his name, her head hanging. All the anger had suddenly drained away. Now she felt just empty.

'Oh. He's still asleep. In any case, I don't think it's

a good idea right now, Mia, do you? He's – well, he's not able – ready yet – to help – but I will, you know that. Shall I walk with you for a bit? I can carry the baby and give you a rest, or I'll take him for an hour, if you like, and you can have a walk by yourself. Give him a feed and then he'll be all right for a little while.' She talked fast, as if she were nervous.

Not like Annie to sound like that. Then Mia realized: of course, Annie was protecting her son. Nothing must spoil things for Will. Ruin his chances. No way was Annie going to let Mia into the house, shrieking and yelling and making a scene.

Mia turned abruptly. She started walking back down the hill. *Horrible woman. She was as bad as the rest of them. Said she'd help, but she wouldn't really. She'd always put Will first, before her, before Kai. Well, stuff her. She'd blown it now. I won't let her have anything to do with Kai ever again. She could take back her stupid baby sling. And all the other baby things.*

She'd had it with everyone.

No one understood.

Nowhere for her to go.

She couldn't even get a bus to Ashton on a Sunday.

She was trapped.

She knew Annie would be watching her, anxious, but she was determined not to look round. When Mia put her finger in Kai's mouth to stop his bleating, he tried to suck it. Gave up when no milk came. The bleats turned to a wail. Perhaps if she walked fast enough, the movement would calm him down. But the weight of him in the baby sling pulled her neck, made her shoulders and back ache, even though he was so small.

Like having a stone round your neck.

Weighing you down.

Left you gasping for air.

Drowning.

## CHAPTER NINE

She'd have to find somewhere to stop so she could feed him and make him shut up. Mia trudged along the beach, looking for some shelter, something to lean against, a place to hide. There was nothing at the Whitecross end, so she kept on going in the direction of Ashton, along the thin stretch of beach left by the high tide. Extra high: a spring tide. It was hard work, walking on pebbles and stony sand into the wind, the baby round her neck dragging her down. His face was a horrible reddy-purple from screaming so much. He'd got himself into such a state he wouldn't be able to feed now.

She walked for miles, it seemed; the beach was totally exposed, no shelter anywhere. Near Stonegate, the old slipway offered a little protection from the wind. Mia slumped down against the rough stone wall and finally undid the sling, and could stretch her neck and shoulders. Kai's face was screwed up in hunger and fear. Instead of it moving her to softness,

Mia just felt irritation. She handled him roughly, so he cried more, and arched away from her when she finally unzipped her jacket so he could feed.

'Don't, then,' she snapped. 'See if I care.'

She closed her eyes for a moment and leaned back. Kai squirmed and shrieked on her lap, but the wind took his cries away, mixed them with the cries of the gulls, the shushing of the waves pulling back the shingle, so that the sound gradually became less grating on her nerves and for a moment she could rest.

Sunlight reflecting off a can caught the baby's attention. He stopped crying to watch the bright light. He stretched his hand out as if to clutch it.

Mia heard the church clock strike twelve. Dad would be furious. He and Mum would have had to spend time alone together, waiting for her and Kai to return. *Let them wait.*

She began to feel a bit better. She bent over the baby, touched her face against his. He turned avidly, his mouth opening like a hungry baby bird. 'Silly boy.' Mia held him close to her, showed him where to find her breast. She watched the waves, lulled by their gentle slide and suck on the pebbles. Two small birds flitted from rock to rock down near the water. She tried to remember what Will had called them, last summer.

Pipits. That was it. Rock pipits. He was full of useless information like that. No good to her, though, was it? She tried to imagine him sitting with Ali on the beach. Couldn't. Ali hated the beach. He'd soon find out. They didn't have anything in common. Ali liked shopping and clubs and older men who had money to spend on her. They didn't even like the same music.

But, then, what had she had in common with him, either? Becky used to say it was because she was so different that Will had liked her in the first place. She was exciting, and dangerous. And fun.

Not any more.

A girl with a baby.

No wonder he didn't want her.

Voices, people coming down the path from Stonegate to the beach. Mia got up, stiff from sitting in the cold so long. She held Kai against her shoulder. He'd fallen asleep at last. She walked back along the beach with him like that, his breath warm on her neck. Her arms ached, but she couldn't bear to wake him up again to put him back in the horrid sling. In the end, she left it behind on the beach. She didn't want it. It could join all the other rubbish on the tideline.

By the time she got to Whitecross she was beginning to regret it. Kai seemed to get heavier as she went along, and she was scared she might stumble and drop him. His delicate head on those stones.

Mum was waiting in the garden in a deckchair. She got up to greet Mia.

'At last! You're back. Are you all right?'

Mia scowled.

'I'm pleased you've been out, love. Honestly. I'm sure it's good for you. But you were quite a long time. You look exhausted. Shall I take him? Put him down in the basket?'

Mia handed over the sleeping baby. 'I'm going to lie down.'

'Of course. Good idea. Lunch will be ready soon. Dad's in the kitchen now. Just tell him you're back. He worries, you know.' She smiled, shrugged apologetically. 'A parent's privilege. You understand.'

'No, I don't.'

Mia stomped upstairs without looking into the kitchen.

It was a relief to lie down alone on the soft bed. The thought of having to talk to Mum, answer questions, all that! She wanted to sleep, but couldn't. Too many thoughts whirled round her head. Will. Ali. Becky. All the mothers, poking their noses in the whole time. Dad fussing. And Kai. Only thirteen days old and so needy she couldn't bear it. The thought of this going on and on, days and months and years of it.

No wonder her own mother had left.

The image of the abandoned baby sling came into her head. The small heap of blue cloth on the cold pebbles, getting steadily smaller as she walked away.

A dot on the beach. Flotsam and jetsam.

Someone combing the tideline, searching for shells, treasures, might find it, pick it up, take it home. It might come in useful. Would need a bit of a wash, but that's all. Or maybe not. The sea would find it first, waves licking up, round, sucking it back, rolling it over and over until it was sodden and heavy and waterlogged. It would bob out to sea, deeper, further, and then some few days later it might be spewed up again on another beach, a thin ribbon of shredded cloth.

'More potatoes?'

'No.'

'You've hardly eaten anything, Mia.'

'Not hungry.'

'You have to eat, love, when you're feeding a baby. You'll wear yourself out. Then you won't have enough milk for him.'

'I know all that. Stop going on at me.'

Mum sighed. She turned to Dad. 'Lovely lunch, David. I really enjoyed being cooked for. Thanks.'

'Doesn't Bryan cook, then?' Mia smirked.

'Are you being deliberately difficult, Mia?' Mum's voice was pinched with the effort of holding on to her temper.

'You know me! I was born like it.'

'Just stop it, you two! You're spoiling my meal.'

'Sorry for breathing. I'll leave you to it, then.'

'Mia! We haven't finished. There's pudding still to come. Sit back down!'

'Not hungry. I told you. I'm going to make the most of Kai sleeping.'

Mia saw her parents exchange glances.

Dad spoke. 'OK. You can have pudding later. Blackberry crumble.'

Mia left the door ajar, so she could hear their voices from the sitting room, where she was sprawled on the sofa. Mum's voice was clipped with irritation.

'It's impossible to help her. She's so stubborn. And spiky. Rude.'

'She's sixteen, Alice. Remember?'

'How on earth is she going to manage? She's much too immature for this huge responsibility. We should never have let it get this far.'

'*We?* I don't recall there was much of an option. She made her own decision. Eventually. Anyway, it's too late for saying this now, Alice. We've just got to get on with it. She's doing well, really. If you think about it. She's looking after Kai. Feeding and nappies and everything.'

'Well, it's just a novelty at the moment. What happens when she gets tired of it? Because she will. She's never been able to stick at things. Not as a little girl. Not now.'

'It's not like playing a musical instrument or something. This is a relationship.'

'Exactly.'

'What do you mean by that?'

'Well, she's hardly made a success of those, has she?'

'That's pretty unfair. Look who's talking.'

'David! How dare you!'

'Well. Leave off Mia. She's got enough on her plate.'

'I'm just worried about her. And that baby. Their future.'

'Well, don't. *We're* managing. Quite well, thank you very much.'

Mia listened while her parents tried to steer their way out of the argument. They always ended up like this. Still getting at each other, after all these years. But at least Dad had stood up for her. She *was* doing OK. So was he. She thought, guiltily, of her anger with Kai that morning. The baby sling she'd left lying on the beach. It was only a moment, though, wasn't it? She had fed him, eventually, and kept him warm, and now he was sleeping deeply, none the worse for his morning.

She went over to the basket and peeped in. His mouth quivered as he slept, and one fist opened and closed. Do babies dream? Perhaps he was dreaming now.

Two presents were stacked on the floor near the French windows. Mia picked up the large one. She tore the paper a bit, to see what was inside. Disposable nappies. She read the label. Mum had written: *Hope these help. I've arranged a regular supply to be delivered. Not good for the planet, I know. Still, they do make life easier.*

The other parcel was small, hard. It, too, was addressed to Mia, so she opened it, even though she knew she should have waited till Mum actually gave it to her.

*Brilliant! A mobile phone!*

She must have been the only person in the entire universe who didn't already have one.

Mia looked up as Mum came into the room. 'Thanks. It's great.'

'I thought it would come in handy. When you leave the baby with people, you know, and want to check in and see he's all right. That sort of thing. Or if Dad needs to get in touch. When you're out and about more.'

Mia's face fell. She'd been imagining long conversations with Becky, or Tasha, or – well – stupid though it seemed, even with Will. That was why you needed a mobile. Not for *babysitting*.

'I know David doesn't really approve, but you're sixteen now. And I know how useful mine is.'

'Yes.'

'Sorry about the arguing. We just don't seem able to get out of the habit. However, let's not spoil the rest of the day. I don't suppose you want a walk now, do you?'

'No.'

'I wanted to go up the fields, you know? To the old barn. Where we used to go when you were small. Where the swallows nest.'

'House martins.'

'What?'

'House martins, not swallows.'

'Well, whatever. Shall I take Kai when he wakes up?'

'If you want.'

'You'll have to show me how to unfold the buggy. I saw it in the hall. It looks complicated. Where did that come from?'

'Becky's mother. Second-hand. Horrible colour.'

'Well, that doesn't matter, does it?'

'Yes, it does. I don't want him to have horrible things. Cast-offs. I want him to have new stuff.'

Mum sighed again, one of her deep, exasperated sighs. But she didn't speak, that was one good thing. She stopped herself just in time.

Dad went with Alice for the walk. Pushing Kai, who looked too little in the buggy, even though they'd made it flat so he could lie down properly, like in a proper pram. Mia watched them leave the garden from her bedroom window.

From here, they looked like ordinary grandparents. Could even be the parents themselves, with their own late-born baby. People their age did have babies, sometimes.

She opened the instructions for the mobile and started to work out how to programme in the numbers of all her friends.

She tried Becky first. No answer. Tasha next.

'Mia! How are you?'

'OK.'

'What're you doing?'

'Nothing much.'

'How's the baby? Becky told us his name. Sweet!'

'Kai's fine. My dad and mum have just taken him out.'

'Why don't you come over, then? Becky's here. Siobhan's probably coming later.'

'Can't. There are no buses on Sundays. Anyway, I won't be able to leave Kai that long.'

'Bring him with you, then. Get your dad to give you a lift.'

Mia snorted. 'Him? As if! Anyway, my mum's visiting us. I suppose she might drop me off when she goes. On her way back to Bristol.'

'Great.'

'I'm on my new mobile. Present from Mum.'

'About time. Join the rest of the human race. I thought your dad wouldn't let you?'

'He didn't know.'

'See you later, then. Give us a ring to say what time. It's a bit of a muddle here, but you won't mind, will you? The kids are over for the day.'

In the background Mia could hear Becky's voice call out, 'Hi, Mia.' She wasn't angry, then. Good.

'See ya!' Just before Tasha pressed the phone off, Mia heard laughter, a babble of voices.

Now she had something to look forward to. One good thing out of the day, at least. Tasha's home was crowded and noisy and welcoming. So long as Ali wasn't there. Tash hadn't mentioned her.

She and Kai could have a lift back with Becky. Better think about what to take with her. Nappies and stuff. She'd find that changing bag someone from Dad's school had given her and put all the stuff in that. And a change of clothes, in case he did one of those enormous yellow poos that squirted out of the sides of the nappy. Disgusting.

She spent ages deciding what to wear. Nothing seemed quite right. Too tight round her waist. Baggy jeans and a sweatshirt would have to do. She'd have to ask Dad for some money and get some new things. They hadn't had a proper talk about money for ages.

Downstairs in the kitchen, Mia eyed the dish of blackberry crumble on the table. She was starving. Hadn't wanted meat and vegetables at lunch time. She spooned herself a large helping into her favourite blue pudding bowl and took it out into the garden to eat.

It was just like the old days. Just her. Pity Will couldn't see her now, like this. He'd soon realize his mistake with Ali. Probably had already.

She thought about Kai, asleep in the ghastly maroon buggy, oblivious to the significance of the walk with his grandparents up to the barn. It hadn't escaped her, though. It was the walk Mia always wanted to do with Dad after Mum left them when Mia was so little. She'd associated it with her mother; something to do with those birds who came back each year to the same nesting sites. All the way from North

Africa, across the sea even, to the place where they'd been born. She'd not understood then, at six, that her mother would not be coming back to live with them at their house. Not ever.

She heard the sound of their feet, almost running, before she saw them. Mia stood up, alarmed. There was Kai, red-faced, bawling against Dad's damp shoulder. Mum followed behind, almost as red-faced, pushing the empty buggy.

'He didn't like the bumpy ground. I think he must be hungry. He woke up when we started going over the field. Sorry, Mia.'

Dad handed over the crying baby. His squirming body felt unfamiliar, as if that small oasis of time alone had changed her.

'I'd forgotten,' Mum was saying, although Mia was hardly listening, too intent on trying to get Kai latched on the right way. He was desperate, gulping in too much air. 'They won't be comforted by anyone but their mother at that age, will they? That's why it's so exhausting!' Mum sank back on to a chair as if she were the exhausted one. She looked almost ready to cry.

'I'll make us all some tea.' Dad disappeared into the kitchen.

Mia seized her moment.

'Can I have a lift to Ashton when you go? To Tasha's?'

Mum still looked dazed. 'Well, yes, I guess so – with Kai, you mean?'

Mia gave her a withering look. 'Of course. I can hardly leave him behind, can I?'

'But how will you get back?'

'Becky's mum will be picking her up. I can get a lift.'

'OK.'

'So, when are you leaving?'

'Five-ish. It's a long drive back. I've got work tomorrow.'

Mum looked hurt. Mia didn't care. Why should she pretend? She'd got nothing to say to her mother. It was all very well her turning up to visit, bringing presents and everything, but she'd never make up for what she'd done all those years ago. How could she think it would ever be all right again?

Mia scooped Kai up and turned him round. She felt how his tensed-up little body had gone soft now, relaxed and warm against her skin. How much he needed her. Such a strange feeling, that it had to be her.

'Cup of tea?' Dad put the mug down on the side table where Mia could reach it.

'Mum's giving me a lift to Tasha's later.'

'What? You're not going out again. For heaven's sake, Mia.' He looked despairingly at Alice. 'It's been a long day already. She was up at the crack of dawn.'

'I've got to have some sort of life,' Mia snapped. 'Got to see my friends sometime.'

'Yes, but – Kai?'

'He'll be OK. As long as he can feed and stuff. I've packed a bag with everything.' There was no way she was going to let him stop her.

Mum gave Dad one of those looks. *Let it go*, it said. *Don't let's start arguing again.*

When they left, just before five, Dad watched from the gate without waving.

## CHAPTER TEN

*M*um drove in silence for a while. Mia sat in the back with Kai strapped into his special baby seat. Brand new – another present from Mum. It had a handle so you could lift the whole thing out and use it like a cradle to carry him around.

Every so often, she saw Mum check her out in the rear-view mirror.

'He's calmed down now.'

'Yes.'

'Perhaps he likes the car. Babies often do.'

'Yes.'

'I didn't have one, when you were small.'

Mum waited for a lorry at the junction with the main road.

'So. How are you feeling? Really.'

'OK.'

'Do you think you're going to manage all this?'

Mia didn't bother to answer.

'We need to sort out money. Has David mentioned it?'

'No.'

'There are benefits and things you are entitled to. You'll have to find out. Apply.'

'Dad used to give me my child allowance.'

'But I don't think he'll get that any more for you. Now you're sixteen. You have to be in education full-time.'

Mia looked out of the window. Mum's voice droned on and on.

'. . . so Bryan and I discussed it again, but I really don't think it's the answer. It's a very small room –'

'Shut up about it, Mum. We already decided, didn't we? It wouldn't work. I don't want to live in Bristol, anyway.'

'But your father may be needing his space too, Mia. He told me about Julie.'

'What about her?'

'He sounded quite – well, serious about her. What's she like?'

'She's a teacher, isn't she?'

'How old is she?'

'How do I know? Youngish.'

'What – twenties? Thirties?'

'I dunno. Twenty-five or something.'

Mum's lips went into a tight line. 'Pretty?'

Mia shrugged. 'A bit tarty, actually. Loads of make-up, short skirts, heels. You know? You're not *jealous*?' She laughed, cruel.

'No, of course not. Just – well – curious.'

*How* sad *could you get?*

They were on the outskirts of Ashton now, not far from the school.

'Do you miss it?'

'What?'

'The school.'

Mia looked out at the flat-roofed buildings, the vacant windows. The flowering cherry trees that bordered the drive were almost over, heaps of browning petals littering the path.

'No way. I hated it. You know I did. I'm not like Laura and Kate.'

'I know. But it might be easier than – well – what you're doing now. Looking after a baby twenty-four hours a day. Don't you miss your friends?'

'Of course I do. But that's all.'

'You might change your mind later. When you've been doing this for a few months. Years.'

They'd arrived in Tasha's street now, a line of terraced brick houses with small front gardens.

'Which one's Tasha's?' Mum asked.

'Number thirty-two. With the blue door. And all the junk in the garden.'

'There you are, then. Let me get your bag for you.'

'It's OK. I can manage.'

She didn't want Mum coming into Tasha's house. She didn't want to see the disapproval register on Mum's face. She'd hate the mess, turn up her nose at the muddle of shoes and coats and bags dumped in the hall, the background babble of a television permanently on in the living room. Mum would completely miss the important things about Tasha's house: how you could just sit about and relax there, didn't have to be doing stuff all the time, didn't have to answer questions.

'OK, then. Bye.' Mum gave Kai a kiss on the head and rubbed Mia's shoulder. 'Good luck. Phone me if you need anything. Money, whatever.'

'I need some money now, actually. Haven't brought any.'

'Mia! You are the limit! Supposing you'd needed something for the baby. Or a taxi to get back. Anything might happen. You have got to start acting more responsibly now!'

Alice fumbled in her bag and fished out her purse. 'Here you are. Twenty pounds cash, and if you can wait a minute I'll write you a cheque, for later.'

Mia watched, open-mouthed, as Mum wrote out a cheque for a hundred and fifty pounds.

'There. Get some new clothes for yourself. Yes?

And promise me you'll take money with you when you go out, always. Enough for emergencies for Kai, at least.'

Mia stuffed the cheque into the baby bag, next to the wipes. 'OK. Thanks. And for the mobile. And the nappies.' She kissed Mum's cheek.

Suddenly Mia felt a whole lot better.

Becky, Tasha and Siobhan were in the kitchen, eating toast.

'Want some?'

Mia shook her head.

'None of us have eaten all day. After last night.' Siobhan laughed. 'I've never been so hungover.'

'You all right?' Becky asked Mia. 'You look a bit spaced-out.'

'My mum's just given me a hundred and fifty quid.'

'You lucky thing. Can I help you spend it?' Becky grinned. 'You should see *Alice* more often, shouldn't you?'

'Who's Alice?' Siobhan asked.

'Mia's mum. That's what she's supposed to call her these days.'

'Kai was miserable. And Mum and Dad argued, as always.'

'He's not miserable now, are you, sweetie-pie? That's cos you like being with us, isn't it?'

'He looks so sweet with his little face peeping out. Can I hold him?'

They passed him round. This time, he didn't seem to mind.

'We missed you at the party,' Tasha said.

A hush went round the table, everyone suddenly watching Mia more closely.

Mia felt her face go hot. 'It's OK, Becky's told me about Will.'

They all started talking at once, reassuring her. *It doesn't mean anything. He doesn't really like her. It's because they were pissed.*

'It won't last,' Siobhan said.

'And how would you know?'

'It's obvious. She's been after him for ages and he's never been interested before. He was feeling bad – got legless –'

'That doesn't make it any better.' Mia's eyes were prickling with tears. 'It's worse, really. That he'd do that and not even like her.'

'He might *like* her, but not mean to go out with her.'

'Where is she, anyway? Has anyone heard from her?'

'No.'

'We don't want to, anyway. Not now. We're on your side.'

'What was she wearing?'

'That black dress. And her hair loose. She did look amazing.'

'Tasha! She looked a right slapper, if you really want to know.'

'Becky!'

'Well, she did. And I shan't forgive her. She knew you'd be gutted.'

'She might not,' Mia said quietly. 'It's not as if we've been together for months now.'

'But you only have to use the tiniest bit of imagination to work it out.'

'That's precisely what she hasn't got. Imagination. She only ever thinks about herself.'

'Ah, look at Kai!' Tasha said. 'The way his mouth's going in and out!'

'Cute!'

'He's hungry.'

'No, he isn't.'

'How do you know, Mia?'

'I just do.'

'Who's revised for the French oral, then?'

'You can't revise for an oral exam.'

'Yes, you can. Vocabulary and stuff. Practise saying things.'

Becky groaned. 'My mum'll make me when I get back tonight.'

'Ali's probably been revising all day,' Siobhan giggled. *'Je t'aime, tu m'aimes –'*

'Shut up!' Becky hissed.

Mia sat at the kitchen table with Kai on her lap, head bent low so they wouldn't see her tears. It wasn't just about Will. It was all the talking that left her out. Already it was happening. They were moving on, away. Soon she'd be left far behind, her and Kai.

There was the sound of voices, and then the kitchen door pushed open and Billie, Tasha's half-sister from London, came in. She held her youngest child straddled on her hip. The little girl's black hair was all fluffed up at the back where she'd been sleeping on it. She sucked her thumb and looked with big eyes at the girls round the table.

Billie's eyes lit up. 'Mia! Your baby! Oh, look! So gorgeous. Tiny!' She shifted the weight of her own child on to her lap as she sat down next to Mia. 'Look, Lily. A newborn baby! Isn't he lovely?'

Lily stretched out her hand and gently smoothed Kai's head. Her brown skin made Kai's look too pale, Mia thought. As if he were ill.

'Baby,' Lily said.

'That's right. What's his name, Mia?'

'Kai.'

'Oh, that's just gorgeous. I've never heard that before, that name.'

Mia flushed. 'It means "man of the sea".'

Billie laughed loudly. 'Well, he'll grow into that. And how're you doing, Mia?'

'OK. Mostly.' Her voice sounded thin, pale like Kai's skin, in contrast to Billie's.

'Make us tea, then, Tasha.'

Billie's bright presence filled the kitchen. Having her there, and Lily, changed the balance. Mia started to feel more cheerful again. She settled down with her mug of tea to answer Billie's questions about the birth, and so she hardly noticed when the other girls drifted away from the table, into the lounge, and started to watch the telly.

She was still there when Becky's mother turned up to take them home. She and Becky chatted in the car, and Kai slept, and when she got home even Dad seemed in a better mood.

## CHAPTER ELEVEN

Crouched on the bathroom floor, Mia was changing Kai's nappy. He kept kicking his legs: one little bare foot caught the edge of the old nappy and smeared poo over the clean Babygro.

'Keep still!' she hissed. She felt herself get hotter. How come he was being so difficult today? She grabbed his legs harder than she meant to and he whimpered.

At last she got him neatly parcelled up. She leaned back on her heels, breathed out with relief. She hadn't meant to be so cross. She bent over him and blew raspberries on his tummy. His eyes lit up and his hands waved like tiny propellers. She left him there on the floor while she went to find another Babygro in the bedroom. The last clean one left in the drawer; she'd have to put the washing machine on before she left. And there wouldn't be any spare clean things to take out with her. Why did everything have to be so complicated? It had taken hours already, just to get ready to catch a bus to Ashton to go to some stupid meeting.

She still had to feed him, and then, just as she set foot out of the door, you could guarantee he'd do another huge poo, or sick his feed up on his clothes, or hers. And how was she supposed to get herself ready, when he so hated to be left lying in his basket, or anywhere, when he was awake? She looked awful. Hadn't washed her hair for days.

How did other people manage? They left the baby to cry, she supposed, or had someone to help hold him, or maybe they just didn't go out.

Finally, they made it to the bus stop. She had to run the last bit, the bus already visible on the straight main road into Whitecross, and was out of breath by the time she got to the stop.

An elderly man waiting at the stop helped her fold the buggy up and carry it on to the bus. The driver tutted impatiently at them for taking so long. Mia held out the twenty-pound note from Mum.

'No change,' he said unhelpfully.

Mia held Kai against her shoulder. He was beginning to whimper. 'It's all I've got,' she said.

Stalemate.

Behind her, the old man sighed, felt in his pocket and leaned forwards to Mia. 'Here, have this.' He handed her a two-pound coin.

'Thanks. I'll get change at the bus station. Pay you back.'

She turned back to the driver. 'Child return to Ashton.'

'You don't pay till they're five.'

'No, for me.'

'You what? How old are you?'

'Sixteen.'

'That's full fare unless you've got a student pass. Which you haven't.'

She'd forgotten. Hadn't been on a bus since her sixteenth birthday. Humiliated, she sank into the front seat. The driver was still muttering under his breath: *Bloody teenagers with babies. Whatever next?* Mia stared, hard, out of the smeared window, trying not to hear. The lime trees were almost in flower. She could see the clusters of tight yellow buds.

The old man smiled at Kai every so often.

'Keep the money,' he told Mia when they got to Ashton bus station and he'd carried the buggy off for her. 'Have it for the babby. It's lucky to give money to a new babby.'

As soon as she got to the health centre she wished she hadn't come. That smell. The beige carpet tiles, low-level chairs arranged in a square around the edges of the waiting area.

The woman at reception looked Mia up and down. 'You want upstairs,' she said. 'Young Parents.'

Mia nodded.

How was she supposed to get upstairs with the buggy? She hovered, trying to think how to do it, when two girls in identical silver puffa jackets pushed through the swing doors. Mia watched them unstrap their babies in turn, fold and park up their buggies, still deep in conversation with each other, and go upstairs.

She did the same with Kai, but it was too hard to fold the buggy without anyone to hold him for her, and in the end she left it as it was, taking up too much space.

She hovered in the doorway, ready to bunk off: one look had told her that it was too like school. She'd be the new girl. They were all chatting in groups, drinking coffee, laughing. But Vicky had already spotted her.

'Come on in, Mia. Coffee? Juice? Hello, Kai. Doesn't he look wonderful? He's so bright and alert!' She beamed at Mia. 'Well done! And for getting here.'

There was one girl standing by herself, looking out of the window. Long dark wavy hair, dark skin, a strikingly beautiful face. She held herself aloof, as if she didn't want to be there at all. Mia took it all in: the grace and poise of the girl, her straight back. *Like a dancer,* she thought. And then, *That must be the girl Vicky mentioned before.*

'She's been poorly,' Vicky said quietly. 'She doesn't really know anyone here yet.' She looked at her watch. 'We ought to get started. It's a time to chat, ask questions, find out how the other mums cope with things. That's the most useful part, really. Sometimes we have a speaker, or I give a bit of information. We'll do names, so you can get to know everyone.'

Mia sat down in one of the empty chairs. The girl still stood at the window, her baby in her arms, talking to him in a low voice.

'Come and join us, Colleen. There's a spare seat next to Mia,' Vicky called out.

One of the other girls giggled. Mia watched Colleen turn, dazed, as if she'd forgotten where she was, why she was here. She flushed when she realized everyone was looking at her. Poor thing. Mia knew just how that felt. She tried to look sympathetic by smiling, but Colleen's face stayed taut, suspicious.

Mia wished she hadn't come. Sitting in a circle of chairs, going round saying names, yours, then the baby's: excruciating. She blushed when it was her turn, expecting someone to giggle. Her voice sounded squeaky and pathetic. There were eight girls altogether. No one looked older than about eighteen.

Jenny, Lisa, Rosie, Sharon ... Colleen's voice when she spoke was surprisingly clear; she'd pulled herself together.

Vicky announced the day's topic: 'Enjoying your baby'. A couple of the girls laughed.

'Give us a break!' someone called Mel squawked out.

Mia recognized her as one of the girls in the silver jackets. Vicky smiled, but she kept going. Mia's thoughts drifted round the room. The babies who'd been placed on the carpet in the middle of the circle squirmed and wriggled like fat little grubs. Mia held a sleepy Kai on her lap; Colleen held her baby, too. He looked tiny. From time to time she whispered to him, reassuring him, explaining things. It reminded Mia of the way Vicky talked to the babies.

'What's his name? I didn't catch it,' Mia whispered to Colleen.

Vicky was saying something about babies loving books. She was winding up her talk now.

'Isaac.' Still she didn't smile.

Mel and Sharon started collecting up the cups.

'Who wants another? Put the kettle on, someone,' Mel called out.

The girls looked comfortable here, laughing and chatting about the babies, whether they'd got what they wanted.

'I wanted a boy, but now I'm really glad I've got her. My Dave wanted a girl all the time.'

'There's nicer clothes for the girls, anyway, aren't there?'

'I hope the next one's a boy, though.'

*Next one? What planet was she on?*

'How old is yours?' Mel was asking Mia.

'Two and a bit weeks.'

'Ahh. He's sweet. Mine's nearly six weeks, except he was early, so really he's about four weeks, if you see what I mean. He's already sleeping through. Is yours?'

She was trying to be kind, letting Mia in. But Mia felt, as she so often did, cross and resentful, not wanting to be part of the club. She knew girls like this at school, cosy and chatty and totally boring. Sort of middle-aged, even before they were sixteen. Having a boyfriend, having babies, that was all they wanted, they said. Though who was she to judge now?

Vicky had moved to an empty seat next to Colleen. They were talking in low voices and Vicky had taken the baby on to her lap. Colleen's face looked cagey, almost afraid.

The baby was very small. Mia tried to remember what Vicky had said about Colleen before, something about her being ill and about not knowing anyone.

Vicky turned round. 'Mia? Have you met Colleen yet?'

She nodded. 'Sort of.'

'Colleen's only been once before to the group. So you're both new! I'll leave you to it.'

They watched Vicky walk over to the counter, where most of the other girls were now standing, spooning instant coffee into mugs, babies balanced on hips or over one arm like seasoned experts.

'She's nice, isn't she?' Mia said.

'Yes.'

Mia rummaged for something else to say. It wasn't like her to make such an effort. Especially when someone was trying so hard to get her to be friendly. Even if it was Vicky. But there was something about Colleen, something that made Mia persist. Her difference from the other girls, perhaps. The sense of a possible kindred spirit.

'What did you think of it? The group?' Mia asked.

'Not much.'

'Me neither. It's just like school, isn't it? PSHE lessons.'

'What's that?'

'You know, personal and health social something or other. Schools have to do it. About sex and drugs and stuff. Doesn't your school?'

'I don't go to school.'

'Well, no, not now –'

'Not before him, either. Well, only now and then. Here and there.'

There was an uncomfortable pause.

'Lucky you,' Mia said.

Colleen looked at her sharply.

'I didn't like school much,' Mia explained.

'Why not? Didn't you like learning stuff?' Colleen sounded shocked.

It was hard for Mia to explain. She didn't think about school in terms of learning stuff. Being told what to do, being judged, criticized, failing. Being bored. Miserable. That was what school had been about for her.

'Why didn't you go to school, then?' Mia asked instead.

Colleen shrugged. 'Moving about too much.'

Mia remembered, suddenly, what Vicky had told her. Travellers. The fair.

Colleen's face had closed up again.

The other girls were picking up their babies, wrestling them into little coats and zip-up bags, getting ready to leave.

'There's a cafe in the market I go to sometimes,' Mia said. 'Do you want to come?'

Colleen shook her head. 'Got to go.'

Disappointed, Mia watched through the window

as Colleen left the health centre and walked up the street. She lugged the baby in her arms wrapped round in an old woollen blanket. Every so often she stopped, said something to him, shifted him round. Mia watched till they were out of sight.

She put Kai back in the buggy and pushed it out into the damp street. What now? The whole afternoon stretched ahead. She headed for the market cafe by herself. At least it would be warm in there. She could get a burger or something, and feed Kai.

When she got there it was crowded with shoppers having all-day breakfasts. There was a large group of women on some sort of a day out, not the sort of women who normally ate there. Their voices were too loud, their clothes all wrong. Too smart, or fashionable, or something. They were laughing at one of the women for having chips, as if it were some sort of big deal. Mia fed Kai while she waited for her toasted sandwich, turned away from the other shoppers. She hated the way people tried to watch.

Afterwards, Mia went back through the precinct to the bus station. It was a long wait for a bus that went all the way to Whitecross. In the end, she got on one that dropped her off at Stonegate. She had to feed Kai sitting in the bus stop before she began the long walk the rest of the way home. She had to go along the main road almost all the way, and for a long stretch of it there wasn't even a pavement. Cars had to swerve out past her and the buggy. Several blasted their horns as they zoomed past. *Ignorant pigs!*

She thought about Colleen again and felt cross with herself for not handling it better with her. It would have been nice to meet up again. She liked the way Colleen had talked to her baby. And the way she looked. And then remembering what Vicky had said about her, that she'd been travelling with the fair, well, that just made her more exciting, somehow. Someone different and interesting. And with a baby, like her. Perhaps another time. If she went to the group next week. Though she doubted that Colleen would go again. Perhaps Vicky would say something. Give her a phone number.

Dad was already back from school by the time Mia got home. She'd dawdled along the road once she'd got to the village, hoping she might see someone from school, but they must be finishing at odd times now that the exams had started. Kai slept in the buggy.

'Everything all right?' Dad looked up from the table and his pile of papers.

'Yes.'

'You look exhausted. What've you been up to today?'

'That meeting in Ashton – you know, with Vicky?'

'Oh, yes. The young mums' group.'

'Young *parents*, actually. Not just mums.'

'So how many fathers were there?'

'Well, none, actually. But that's not the point.'

'Meet anyone nice?' Dad asked half-heartedly.

'Ish. One girl.'

Dad's attention was back on the papers on the table.

'Colleen, she's called,' Mia said.

'Oh, yes?' Dad frowned slightly.

'From the fair. Travellers.' That got his full attention.

'Mia!' Dad leaned forwards, head in hands.

'What's the matter now?'

'The sort of unsuitable people you always want to get involved with. Please, Mia, do us all a favour.'

'*Us*? What are you talking about? What do you mean *unsuitable*? Just because Colleen travels with the fair! Talk about narrow-minded!'

'Hang on a minute, Mia. Stop overreacting.'

'You're the one overreacting. How can you be-grudge me having *one* friend who might know something about what it's like for me? In any case, I hardly even know her yet. You haven't a clue, have you? You're so old and sad.'

'OK, leave it out. I don't want an argument with you. Just take care, that's all.'

'You think I'm just a child! You even want to control who I'm friends with! You'd rather I was like you and had no friends at all!'

The old rage welled up inside. Mia wanted a proper argument. To be able to shout and slam doors. But Dad wasn't having it.

'How's Kai been today?' He'd changed tack. His voice softened as soon as he spoke about the baby. He even looked different.

Grudgingly, Mia answered him. 'Kai's fine. He's had a good day. Now he's sleeping in the buggy.'

'Good. I'll start supper in a minute, soon as I've finished marking this lot. You go and have a rest.'

Mia took the phone from the hall and went through into the sitting room. She sank down on the sofa, dialled the number.

'Becks?'

'Mia! Did your dad say? I phoned earlier. Haven't got your mobile number. Are you all right? I thought you might want to meet up. After school, Friday. Spend that money from your mum.'

'Not Friday – well, maybe. I might be in town earlier; I could stay on. If Kai's OK. What time are you finishing?'

'Normal time.'

'How was the French exam?'

Becky groaned. 'Terrible. I mucked up.'

'You always say that. You'll be OK. You don't need it, anyway. Not for Textiles and Fashion. Did you see Will?'

'Not properly – well – you know. Not to talk to.'

'Was *she* there?'

'Ali? Yes.'

'With him?'

'Not really. Not so as you'd notice.'

'Meaning?'

'Just like normal. Nothing *special* between them. He's probably regretting it already. Siobhan and Liam are definitely going out. She says he's a really good kisser.'

'I can't imagine it. He's always larking about – you know. Not serious, ever. What does Matt think about it?'

'How should I know? He's hardly speaking to me. Shall we meet up, then?'

'Probably. Yes. I'll have my phone. I'll give you the number. Just in case. Usual place?'

Mia lay back against the sofa cushions. She could smell frying onions and red pepper. Dad was doing his stir-fry special. She still felt angry with him. How dare he say that stuff about her? Well, she'd show him. She'd make a point of seeing Colleen again now.

Kai was still asleep in the buggy, parked in the

hall. It could be an ordinary day, her lounging about, talking on the phone, arranging to meet up with the others. They'd probably be down at the bus stop later, deciding what to do. It would be light till nearly nine thirty. Maybe they'd take some cans down on the beach. Make a fire, even. Liam, Matt, Becky and Siobhan. Will.

But she wouldn't be there, would she? She'd be bathing Kai, and feeding him, and cuddling him to sleep, and then crawling into bed completely shattered, hoping for more than two hours' sleep before he woke again, and fed again, and cried. And all night it would be like that, until he woke bright-eyed at five or six, ready for another day. How on earth was she going to bear it?

## CHAPTER TWELVE

On Friday morning, Mia got the bus into Ashton again. She pushed the buggy round the precinct for a bit, hoping she might bump into someone: Colleen, or someone from school, but there was no one she knew, just the usual dreary crowds of people trailing round shops, and a couple of blokes playing guitars, badly, and some old man talking loudly about Jesus. It didn't feel like late May. The sky was overcast, and a cool wind whipped up small flurries of cigarette ends and discarded paper wrappers and dust. She thought about the park, where the fair camped each holiday. That was the sort of place Colleen might hang out. She'd know it well enough, from being with the fair, and there were benches to sit on. It was as good a place to go as any. Mia could sit on the swings, even, with Kai on her lap. Give him a taste of things to come. She'd always loved the swings as a little girl; that moment when you hang, high, at the top of the swing, before it free-falls back to earth. Eyes open, head back, your head full of sky and air.

Her hunch was right. She found Colleen eventually in one of the wooden shelters in the park, overlooking the bit fenced off for young children, with bark chippings round slides and swings and a wooden construction for climbing over. It was beginning to rain. Colleen had her coat collar turned up; she looked numb with cold.

Mia's heart was beating fast. Perhaps Colleen wouldn't want to speak again. Might not even recognize her from the Wednesday group.

'Hi!'

Colleen gave a small, shy smile. 'It's you, from Vicky's thing, isn't it?'

'Mia. Yes.'

'Want to sit down? It's dry, just about.'

'Thanks. Freezing, isn't it?'

'Better than inside, though. It does my head in sometimes.'

'I know. Me too.'

The rain fell more heavily. Colleen pulled a battered old pram closer, under the shelter.

'You've got a pram, then,' Mia said. 'I wondered, on Wednesday, cos you were carrying him.'

'It's new. Well, not new, obviously. New to us.'

It looked like something from a skip: a battered

blue canvas thing on a metal frame. Colleen didn't seem to mind.

'From Vicky. One of her old mums who didn't need it no more. She said it had done five of hers, but it's still good enough for Isaac. He's warm and dry, anyway.'

*And I'd thought my second-hand buggy was bad!*

Isaac began to whimper. Colleen fished a bottle of milk formula from her bag. 'Wish I didn't have to feed him this rubbish.'

Mia didn't know what to say.

Colleen turned, her eyes fierce. 'It's not what I want, you know. It's only cos I was ill.'

They sat in silence while Colleen fed her baby with the bottle. She held him on her lap, tight against her, her jumper rucked up as if she were breastfeeding. Mia tried not to stare.

'I want him to feel my skin still,' Colleen said. 'Even if he can't have my milk.'

'How old is he?' Mia asked, when it seemed they'd finished the feed.

'Seven weeks. I know he's tiny. He wasn't getting enough. But he's putting on weight now. Vicky's pleased with us.'

'I read something,' Mia said, 'you know, about breastfeeding. You can start again, even if you stop. Even women who adopt babies can sometimes feed them. I know it sounds weird, but it's in this book. I can lend it to you if you want.' She saw the look on Colleen's face and wished she'd kept her mouth shut.

They sat side by side in the wooden shelter, listening to the rain drumming on the roof, each with one hand on the buggy or pram, pushing them to and fro when the babies got fretful, like they'd seen other mothers do. *Real mothers,* Mia thought. *Not like us. It's like we're just pretending.*

Mia could see droplets of water glistening on the chains for the swings; the mown grass held a fine skein of silver. From time to time, Colleen coughed.

What could she say to stop Colleen just leaving again?

'Why don't we go to a cafe? We could warm up a bit.'

'Well, if it's not too expensive.' Colleen sounded anxious.

'I'll pay, if you like. My mum gave me some money when she came down from Bristol at the weekend. She doesn't see me very often. Giving me money makes her feel better.'

Colleen laughed at that, and Mia felt relieved. She hadn't blown it completely yet, then.

'So you're doing her a favour, really, taking her money off her?' Colleen said.

'Exactly.'

'You sound like you don't like your mum much.'

Mia shrugged. 'S'pose. Her fault, though. She left, didn't she?'

Colleen looked at Mia, her face curious. 'What do you mean, left?'

'She left us, when I was little, six. My dad brought us up.'

'Oh.' Colleen stroked her baby's head, smoothed the ruffled dark hair tenderly. 'It's hard to imagine, isn't it? Leaving.'

Mia didn't like to say what she thought. That it wasn't so hard to imagine, not really. Not any more.

'So, will you come to a cafe? If my mum pays?'

'OK. You say where. I don't know many places.'


They found a table in the corner of the market cafe. It was warm and dry, at least, even though it stank of stale hot fat. They got the babies out for a feed. The woman behind the counter warmed the half-drunk bottle for Colleen.

'I've seen you before,' the woman said to Mia. 'You used to come in here a lot, didn't you? And what have we got here?' She leaned further over the counter. 'You've been busy! He's a bonny boy, isn't he?' the woman prattled on.

She brought two plates of buttered toast over to their table. They had only ordered drinks.

'You both look as if you need fattening up!' she fussed. 'Makes me feel old, seeing you with babies. You still look like kids yourselves!'

Colleen seemed more friendly once she'd eaten something and warmed up. Mia wanted to ask her loads of things, stuff about the fair, and the baby and everything, but she daren't. Not yet.

It was nice having someone to be with, not just her and Kai. Not quite so lonely.


It had stopped raining by the time they came out of the precinct. The streets gleamed wet; the sun was coming out.

'Where now?' Mia said.

'Back to the park?'

'Or the river?'

They pushed along the muddy towpath, going side by side where it was wide enough. The wet nettles and cow parsley drooped over the path, drenching their jeans.

'Someone should cut this stuff back,' Mia said.

'No, I love it. It's beautiful. Like real countryside. And all that white hawthorn blossom on the trees.'

*Hawthorn.* She sounded like Will, knowing the names.

'That one there's an ash.' Mia pointed to a huge tree with fresh, newly opened leaves, brilliant green against the grey branches. 'We've got one in our garden. That's how I know.'

'Lucky you, having a garden,' Colleen said. 'I'm staying in a poky flat. Just till I can join Mum again. But there's no garden, not even a balcony. No fresh air. Babies need fresh air. So do I!' She laughed, and her breath caught in her chest, making a wheezy sound.

They pushed a bit further.

'If we keep going,' Mia said, 'we can watch the boat going up the locks on to the canal. And there's a bench there so we can sit down for a rest.'

Kai whimpered in the buggy. He'd had enough of lying still, seeing nothing but sky. Mia got him out when they stopped at the bench, propped him up against her raised knees so he could see her face properly, like Vicky said to do.

'Aren't his eyes blue?' Colleen leaned forwards to look closely. 'But yours aren't.'

'No. He's got his dad's eyes.'

'Like Isaac, then.'

Neither of them had mentioned the dads before. The word hung in the air between them, cleared a space where something might happen.

Mia plunged in. Risked it. 'What's he like, then? Isaac's dad?'

Colleen sighed, then laughed. 'Talented, handsome,

gorgeous in every way. Of course. Why else would I have chosen him? And,' she added wryly, 'a long way away by now! We won't be seeing him again.'

Mia realized she'd been holding her breath, scared she'd gone too far. How different this was from talking to Becky, Tasha, Siobhan. They'd have told Mia everything. She would have insisted on all the details. But it felt like a sort of triumph that Colleen had said this much. She was just about to say something about Will, just to make it fair, when Colleen turned away from the lockside.

'I think I'll go back to my flat now,' Colleen said. 'I need a sleep. You?'

Mia looked at her watch. Ages till her meeting with Becky. 'Nah. I'll stay a bit longer. I'm meeting someone later. A friend, from school.'

'Oh.'

'Shall I see you next week, then? You could come to Whitecross?'

'Where's that?'

'Where I live. A village. It's near the sea. There's a bus.'

Colleen shook her head. 'I'll meet you in the park again, though, if you want.'

'Monday? Tuesday?'

'Whenever.'

'I have to know when, cos of getting the bus in and everything.'

'Monday, then.'

Mia watched Colleen make her way slowly along the path. She walked with a sort of elegance, in spite of the disgusting old pram, which bounced and rattled over the rutted ground, wheels wobbling. Graceful: that was the word.

Mia thought about her some more. When she laughed, her whole body changed. It lit up. And when she talked to her baby, showed him things. She talked to him as if he understood everything, wanted to learn about it. Mia could imagine taking Colleen to the beach at Whitecross. She'd like that. She wondered what she'd been ill with.

She thought of Colleen going back to her flat, all by herself for a whole weekend. And she thought about the house in Whitecross. The garden. Her room, newly decorated by Becky and her.

Why didn't she feel lucky, then? Because she'd always lived there? Took it for granted? Because it wasn't really her house; it was Dad's? Because she felt tied, and trapped, too much a child, in the place she'd always lived? Because being safe, and comfortable, weren't enough? Even now, even with a baby?

*

The day was too long. At last it was time to meet Becky. They went from shop to shop, looking at trousers, and tops, and jackets, and shoes. It didn't seem as much fun as usual.

'What's up, Mia?'

'I'm just tired. I've been in town all day, nearly. And Kai's had enough.'

'Let's get a Coke or something, then. Sit down. I'll push the buggy for a bit.'

'Nah. I think I need to go home.'

'But you haven't bought anything! At least get those jeans you tried on. And one top. The lilac one.'

'I look horrible.'

'No, you don't!'

'I'm still too fat.'

'You're *not*, Mia! That's mad! What does that make me, then? An elephant?'

They laughed. In the end, Mia bought the lilac T-shirt, and the faded denim jeans, and a belt – too expensive, really, but she looked fabulous, Becky said.

## CHAPTER THIRTEEN

Mia woke out of a deep, satisfying sleep. The room was flooded with pearly light, the window a square of pale blue sky. She reached out a hand for the clock on the bedside cabinet: five thirty. She'd slept since eleven. Six and a half hours of uninterrupted sleep! Unheard of! And then came the heart-stopping jolt: *Kai*. Why hadn't he woken her? He'd never slept this long before.

She sat up properly. There was the basket by the bed, and the small mound of cream woollen blanket. He was lying on one side, his cheek curved against the undersheet. For a second she watched him, straining to see the rise and fall of his sleeping breaths, but even then she couldn't be sure, and had to stretch out and touch his cheek, feel that it was warm. He sighed; the fingers on one hand uncurled slightly.

Mia let out her own breath in a long sigh. Cot death. Suffocation. Meningitis ... the list went on and on, all the things you could worry about. If you chose. Silly, really. Worrying all the time. But sometimes you couldn't help it.

Mia lay back down in bed and stretched her body out flat. She felt the luxury of being deeply rested; no aches anywhere. She placed her hands on her belly. Lying flat like this, it felt almost normal. She thought of the new clothes she'd bought with Becky. Where was she going to wear them? And that made her think of Will. It was such a long time since she'd felt his hands on her body.

The sunny morning made everything easier. Dad hummed some ancient Beatles song as he got ready for work. They ate breakfast together for once, Kai in the bouncy seat Becky's mum had brought round at the weekend. She said she'd got it in a car-boot sale, but it looked brand new.

'He can see what's going on now. That'll keep him happy.'

It seemed to work.

'Do you want a lift into Ashton?' Dad asked. 'I don't have to leave so early this morning. No duty or anything, and the Year Elevens are all off.'

She'd be too early, but it was easier than getting the bus by herself. They folded the buggy into the boot and Mia collected up a bag of nappy-changing stuff.

Dad grinned. 'Got enough for a week, by the look of you.'

He switched the radio on and started singing along.

'You're in a good mood,' Mia said. Then she regretted it. Dad immediately started enthusing about Miss Blackman.

'It's like a new lease of life for me, Mia. Hard though it may be for you to understand, there has been something distinctly lacking in my life.'

Right. Like sex, Mia supposed, remembering Miss Blackman's short, tight skirts, low-cut blouses, as she leaned over the boys in her Year Eleven English class. Mia sniffed.

'She's a very interesting young woman, Mia. Widely read. Very mature for her years.'

'Mum asked how old she was,' Mia said.

'Did she? When?'

'Last time she was here. I think she was a bit jealous or something.'

That shut Dad up.

It was only just after nine when Mia got to the park and there was no sign of Colleen. She sat on the swing to wait. The sun was warm already on her back. She tipped the swing back a bit, pushed off with her feet, began to work it up higher and higher. She loved the feeling of stretch in her arms and legs. *All that crouching and bending over you do with a baby*, she thought, *it grinds you down.*

Swinging high made the chains creak and snag. She'd like to go on swinging, high up in the clear air, in the sunlight, forever and ever.

Kai's wails brought her down to earth. Why did he have to spoil everything? She kept on swinging, even though he was working himself up into red-faced, angry crying, just to show him, but it wasn't the same any more and gradually she let the swing wind down until her feet scraped the chippings on the ground.

He couldn't need feeding again already, surely? He was just being stubborn, feeling left out. Perhaps if she got him out he'd stop grizzling.

The feel of his limp warm body, his too-heavy head butting into her neck, softened her and she cuddled him close, her lips brushing his soft head.

'Do you want a swing, too? Come on, then.'

They were still gently swinging together, Kai held tightly on her lap, when Colleen came into view.

'Isn't it a lovely day? At last!' Colleen called out.

Colleen looked stunning in a sea-green sleeveless dress. 'Charity shop,' she told Mia. 'Pure silk. Two quid. Imagine giving it away!'

'Perhaps they were too fat for it or something. Anyway, good thing they did. You look amazing.'

Mia felt hot and dowdy suddenly in her T-shirt and jeans.

'I wish now I'd said I'd go to your place, if it's by the sea. It's too nice to be in a town today,' Colleen said.

'We could still go there if you want. Get the bus.'

'How much?'

'One-sixty return.'

Colleen rummaged through her purse, counting up change.

Mia thought guiltily of the money she'd spent on Friday with Becky. Nearly sixty pounds.

'How will we get the pram on?' Colleen asked.

'Doesn't it fold up?'

They struggled with it, trying to work out how to fold the rusty metal frame. In the end they gave up.

'I'll take it back home and swap it for the sling thing I've got instead. That'll be much easier.'

'I'll come with you, then I'll know where you live.'


It was a tall, gloomy house, not far from the college where Becky was going to do her Textiles course in September.

'I know it's ugly. It's all right inside. It's been divided up into flats,' Colleen explained. 'Vicky told us about it, when I needed somewhere to stay when Mum had to move on and I wasn't well. It's just temporary, till she can have us again.'

Mia held Isaac for her while she went in with the pram. She sat down on the low wall outside, in the concreted front yard. The baby felt strange in her arms. Smaller, lighter, sort of stiff and unyielding. She hoped he wouldn't cry.

Colleen reappeared, flourishing a blue corduroy baby sling. It looked like something out of the ark, the sort of sling Mia's mother might have used way back. But it worked all right, once they'd managed to tie the baby in properly, fasten the long ties round Colleen's back.

'It'll crease your dress up,' Mia said. 'But never mind. It's much better than a pram.'

Colleen looked out of the bus window all the way to Whitecross, noticing things, asking questions. She held Isaac up at the window, too, but he was focused on his mother's face; he didn't know yet about looking *out*.

They stepped off the bus at Whitecross into stillness, heat. The tarmac shimmered.

'Shall I show you the beach first, or do you want to go straight to the house?'

'Oh, the beach, yes! Zak can see the sea for the first time!'

'Zak?'

'Isaac – Zak.'

'Right. I get it. It's nice, suits him.'

Mia frowned as she bumped her buggy along the pebbles. She had to balance Kai against her shoulder with one hand, drag the buggy behind her with the other. He cried every time she tried to put him down in it. Served her right, didn't it? Colleen skipped along, her baby lolling in the sling.

It was one of those perfect May days. The early haze over the water had dissolved; now a clear sky stretched, a pale blue dome, over silk-smooth sea. Tiny waves rippled, broke, frothed on to the pebbles, slid back.

Colleen settled herself down on a pile of larger stones, baby on lap, transfixed. 'So beautiful. So bright!'

Anyone would think she'd never seen the sea before. But, Mia realized, Colleen was seeing everything anew, through Isaac's eyes. It turned everything into a miracle. Even this tatty strip of pebbles littered with rubbish washed up by the tide.

Mia sat down next to Colleen, lifted her T-shirt so Kai could feed, began to relax. When both babies finally fell asleep, they rigged up shade for them with a blanket draped over the buggy. They scooped out a nest in the pebbles and lined it with another blanket for the babies to lie on.

'Like those birds,' Mia said, 'that lay their eggs right on the pebbles.'

'Whose name you don't know,' Colleen teased.

'No. Although Will would. Kai's dad. We might bump into him, even. Then you can ask for yourself.'

*It was possible*, Mia thought. She wondered what he'd make of Colleen. Wished she was wearing something more exciting. She was much too hot, even with the legs of her jeans rolled up.

Mia took off her trainers, hobbled down to the edge of the water and cooled off in the shallows.

'I can do this, though, better even than Will.' Mia showed off, skimming flat stones. *Six in a row!*

'Show me how,' Colleen demanded. She learned fast, was determined. She practised again and again, till she could do it, too. 'We can teach the babies, when they're bigger.'

'You keep saying that. What we can do when they're bigger.'

'Well, I like thinking about it. How it's going to be.'

Mia didn't want to think about anything in the future. There was just here, now. Her head ached when anyone said something about the future.

'Doesn't Kai look pale next to Zak?' she said instead. 'Like he needs more sun on him.'

'He's bigger, though, already. Even though he's younger.'

'That's because he's so greedy. He still feeds all the

time. Even in the night. Except for last night. He slept all the night, till five thirty.'

'Lucky you.'

They lay back on the pebbles, eyes shut against the sun. The sea shooshed and sucked and Mia felt her breathing slowing, going in time with the rhythm of the waves. In. Out.

They ate their lunch outside in the garden. Mia made a salad, and heated up some pizza from the night before, and spread a rug out on the grass under the ash tree. Colleen lay on her back, with Zak on her tummy, staring up through the mesh of branches at the sky.

'Tell me more about Will, then,' she said.

'You might meet him,' Mia said, 'if we go back along the beach later. I'm surprised he wasn't there this morning.'

'I thought you said he was doing exams.'

'Everyone's on study leave now, except when they have to go in for the actual exams.'

'Don't you mind missing them?'

'What, exams? No way! I'm glad.'

'What about later on, though?'

'What about it?'

'Well, won't you want to get a job and stuff?'

'S'pose. I don't know.'

She didn't want to think about any of that now. It was enough, just lying in the sunny garden, with both babies asleep. She thought about Will again.

'I think you'd like him,' she told Colleen. 'He's into music and learning stuff. He's clever like that. But it's not boring when he talks about it. Not like teachers, or my dad. You know?' She thought for a bit and then added, 'But he's not so clever about other things.'

'Like what?'

'He just seems very young, sometimes. And his mum really overprotects him. She's dead keen for him to do well at school. He probably will. Go to university and that.'

'We might be like that, one day, with Zak and Kai,' Colleen said. 'What does he look like, anyway, your Will?'

'Golden. Fair hair, golden skin, blue eyes. *Really* blue. Gorgeous.' Mia sighed.

Colleen laughed. 'You're still mad about him, aren't you?'

'Maybe. Yes. He's not interested, though. Not any more.'

'How do you know?'

'It's obvious.'

'Have you asked him?'

Mia laughed. 'Of course not! Don't be daft.'

'Why's it daft? Seems sensible to me. Anyway, later on, when Kai's bigger, and sitting and crawling and walking and talking, he won't be able to resist him then, will he?'

*Maybe, maybe not.*

Mia didn't say anything. How come Colleen was so – so sort of optimistic and cheerful about everything? And yet Mia herself hadn't given up hope completely. Still had the pebble Will had left behind for Kai that early morning in the hospital. Or maybe it had been for her. He'd done that before, last summer: given her a pebble from the beach, smooth and beautiful, like a blackbird's egg. A sort of promise.

There was still the problem of Ali, of course. She hadn't told Colleen about that. Didn't want her to think badly of Will.

'Tell me about the fair,' Mia said.

'What do you want to know?'

'What it's like, travelling. You know.'

'The best thing is being outside so much. And I love our caravan. It's not big, or posh, like some of the others, but it's got everything we need. And we have fires outside, sometimes, and people play music. Dance, sometimes. My mum's always wanted to dance, ever since she was a little girl, and she had a spell working as a dancer, way back. She taught me, too. And to play.'

'You make it sound really romantic.'

'Well, it's not. It's tough, too, always moving on. People don't like us much. And there aren't as many children now, travelling. And I didn't go to school – well, I tried a couple of times, but it was too hard – not knowing anyone, not knowing the same things people of my age did, so I never fitted in. So I helped Mum instead.'

'Do what?'

'Candyfloss and hot drinks and doughnuts. She used to do the Ferris wheel with her dad, before. But Health and Safety closed it down.'

'I might have seen you. We used to go with Dad. August bank holiday. Laura always got sick in that thing that whizzes you upside down.'

'And it's hard in the winter, putting the rides up, taking them down, your fingers so cold they stick to the metal bolts, and mud everywhere. The lorry wheels churn up the grass. Exhaust stinks out the place. The generators hum all night. And there's the people. The abuse.'

Colleen stroked Zak's feet as he kicked on the rug. He looked like a little frog, his knees bent up. She'd taken off his Babygro so he could get some air to his limbs: the skin in the creases was red and flaky.

Colleen sighed deeply. 'I'm not sure now, though. I've thought about it lots. It's not the best place for a baby. I'm not sure I want him to be always moving on like I did.' She looked round the sunny garden, with its high brick wall along one side and the hedge on the other, the grassy lawn and flower borders, the big ash tree in the middle. 'I want him to have a garden. A safe, quiet place to play. You're so lucky having this.'

'Maybe. But it's different when you've always lived somewhere. I've been here forever! When Dad goes on about when I was here as a baby, what they did, all that, well, it makes me feel as if I'm trapped in something. You want to stay put; I want to escape. Go somewhere different. Start something new.'

'Perhaps we should do a swap! Except I'd miss my mum.'

Colleen picked Zak up and hugged him tight. She sang to him, half under her breath. '"Like a ship in the harbour, Like a mother and child . . ." That's a lullaby she used to sing to me,' she told Mia.

'How come you've got to stay at that flat, instead of joining her?' Mia asked.

'It's only till I'm properly better. I've got to be near the hospital so they can keep an eye on me. I've got one more appointment with the consultant and then, if everything's OK, I can go.'

Mia felt a twinge of sadness. No one stayed.

\*

They dozed and chatted for so long in the garden that there wasn't time to go back the beach way to the village. Mia went with Colleen to show her the quicker way, straight down Church Lane and on to the main road.

As the bus pulled up, Colleen suddenly threw her arms round Mia. 'Thank you! It's been my best day for ages and ages.'

Mia waited while Colleen got on. There was a moment of panic while she searched for the bus ticket, then they remembered Mia still had it in her pocket, luckily. The driver was the same one she'd had the other day, but even his sarcastic comments couldn't dull Mia's feeling of happiness today.

'Come again. Tomorrow, if it's sunny.' She mouthed the words through the window at Colleen.

The bus was already pulling away. She craned to see what Colleen was saying through the smeared glass. She was holding her hands out in some gesture. Or was she just waving?

Never mind. The day had gone really well. She was still smiling as she pushed the buggy back up Church Lane.

## CHAPTER FOURTEEN

'Dad! That woman's not coming round *again*?'

'I told you yesterday, Mia. Don't make out you've forgotten. And I expect you to be civil.'

'Well, I hope you're going *out* this time. Not staying here.'

'I told you. I'm taking her for a meal. At the Wheelwrights' Arms. We won't be back till late.'

That *we*. Mia hated it. *We won't be back till late.* Presumably that meant *that woman* would be staying the night again, then. Angrily, Mia emptied the damp clothes into the washing basket, ready to hang out. They smelled funny: she'd left them in the washing machine all day, forgotten about them. Now they wouldn't dry till the morning. Even though the evening was fine and sun still filled the garden, you could already see the faint perspiration of dew beading the grass.

It was disgusting, the hold that Miss Blackman had on Dad. Why couldn't he see through the make-up and the clothes and the gym-trained body? The hours she must spend getting ready. Becky and Mia had discussed it. Miss Julie Blackman probably wore make-up in bed. You could get it now, Becky said, she'd seen it in a magazine. Make-up specially designed to be worn in your nightie. Or without it, more likely.

That was another thing. The thought of Dad having sex. Well, she wasn't going to think about it. She'd be sick if she did. She untangled the last Babygros and socks from the machine just as a car crunched up the drive. She looked out of the window.

Miss Blackman parked her car and climbed out. She was wearing an immaculate cream sleeveless dress, just above the knee, and gold strappy sandals with heels. Bare, fake-tanned legs. Hair, brushed up to make it look thicker, was a slightly paler shade than two days ago, when she'd last been round. Dad still refused to believe that it wasn't entirely natural.

'It's all the sun we've been having these last two weeks,' he said. 'Brings out the gold lights in it.'

The sun seemed to have brought something new out in Dad, too. He'd started wearing short-sleeved shirts, crushed linen, and he'd bought new thin cotton trousers, quite nice actually, though she wouldn't tell him so. He'd been out twice already this week. He had a shower more often than Mia these days.

Through the kitchen window, Mia watched Miss Blackman walk across the garden, flicking her hair behind one ear, letting it flop elegantly the other side, and smoothing her dress over her perfectly flat stomach. She must have sensed someone watching: she looked at the window self-consciously, gave a little wave to Mia, who glared back. She looked slightly less confident now, Mia noticed with pleasure.

*She is twenty-nine! Dad is forty-seven. What does she see in him?*

Mia kept watching the little scene playing out before her.

Dad went out to greet her. He held Kai in his arms: he must have picked him up from the bouncy chair, where he'd been lying, awake, but contented. *Dad is showing off*, Mia thought, *what a tender, loving grandpa he is*. She watched them. No, it gradually dawned on her, that wasn't it. He was pretending the baby was theirs: his and Julie's. Ugh! It was disgusting! But perhaps there was nothing more attractive to a woman of nearly thirty than a man who could be good with a baby. Like those black and white posters you see in card shops of some naked, muscle-bound man with a tiny baby cradled in his hands.

Kai, *her baby*, was a prop in his seduction drama. How dare he!

They kissed, the baby caught between them.

Mia barged out into the garden, letting the door bang behind her. The noise startled Kai, who gave out a cry, and Dad and Julie sprang apart.

'It's Kai's bedtime,' Mia announced curtly, although it wasn't. He didn't have a bedtime. He slept when he was ready to sleep. It was one of the things Mia and Dad had been arguing about lately.

Mia took Kai from Dad and turned back to the house without speaking to Miss Blackman. Dad would be furious. She didn't care.

She took Kai upstairs, stood at her bedroom window with him still clutched tight in her arms, shaking slightly. She could hear the murmur of voices from the garden, and then two car doors slammed. She watched Julie drive Dad down Church Lane.

He'd not bothered to say goodbye.

She stood there for ages, till Kai began twisting restlessly in her arms. Perhaps she would try putting him to bed. Then she could have a whole evening to herself. That was what Dad had been going on about the other night. 'Babies like routine,' he'd said. 'It makes them feel safe, knowing where they are.'

'But he won't go to sleep till he's ready. He'll just cry,' Mia had said.

'He'll get used to it if you put him down at the same time each night. If he knows you mean business.'

Mia had told Colleen about it afterwards and

Colleen had laughed. 'It's the grown-ups who need the routines,' she'd said, 'so they can get some peace and quiet in the evenings. The babies don't care what time they sleep. And if there's lots of people around to help it's fine. When I was little, there were always loads of people wanting to help hold me, play with me. That's what Mum says.'

*A bit like Tasha's family*, Mia thought now. Billie had baby Lily but there were always other people around – Tasha's mum, and her grandpa, and cousins, and aunties. And life sort of carried on, even with all the children around. They didn't have to be cleared away so the adults could then have a life.

Because that was what Dad seemed to think. Having her and Kai around got in the way of him and Julie having an evening together at the house. And maybe the real point was, she, Mia, was exhausted. There wasn't really anyone wanting to help her.

The evening stretched ahead. Too much time. Just her and Kai.

After she'd fed him and changed him into his nighttime Babygro, the yellow velour one which made him look like a little fluffy duckling, Mia laid him down in the Moses basket. He lay for a while, eyes open, staring up at Becky's mobile of stars dangling from the ceiling. Then he began to whimper.

*Just leave him. He'll get used to it.* Dad's words

echoed in her head. But they competed with Vicky's: *When your baby cries, he's telling you something. He needs something. He needs to know you're listening.*

Mia went to run a bath. His cries got louder, but the sound of the running water drowned him out. She went back to check. His face looked red and hot. He was still crying. He couldn't really need anything, could he? She'd fed him and changed him, and he'd been cuddled almost all day. To have one uninterrupted bath, that wasn't much to ask.

Mia went back into the bathroom and turned on the radio. She left the door open, so he could hear the music, know that she was still there. She found a small bottle of lavender oil on the shelf and dripped it into the running water. That was better; she could already feel herself starting to unwind. She undressed and stepped into the bath.

She lay in the water for ages. When it cooled down too much, she added more, till the tank was empty and it began to run cold. There would be hardly any hot water left for Dad. Good. Served him right. She lay right back and let her head slip under, felt the water lap the sides of her face. Her hair floated out, a small dark halo. She ran her fingers through the soft fringes. Like seaweed.

She thought of Colleen, standing on the edge of the sea on Wednesday afternoon, twirling round in her turquoise dress, her long hair like a dark wave as she spun round without even getting dizzy.

'How do you do that? Without falling over?'

'You have to fix your eyes on a single point. Keep your focus. Whip your head round, like this. You learn it as a dancer.'

She whirled faster, arms stretched out wide, until her foot slipped on the wet pebbles and she lost her balance, toppled, laughing, sprawled out in the shallow water. Mia watched the turquoise silk dress soak up the wet, turn dark as blood, and Colleen's hair swirled out like weed. She lay there, a stranded mermaid, still laughing, letting the waves wash over her.

'Aren't you freezing?'

'Yes. But only cos I was so hot before.'

'You're crazy! Look at you!'

Mia wished Colleen was here now, staying over. Or Becky, or Tasha, or almost anyone. She closed her eyes, dipped deeper, let the water close right over her face. She held her breath for as long as she could. She used to do that with her sister Laura, years ago. Mia could hold her breath longer than anyone she knew. But she was out of practice. She surfaced, spluttering, gulping for air.

Mia reached out a hand for a towel and got out of the bath, dripping all over the floor. She turned the

159

radio off. Silence. Kai must have gone to sleep, then. Dad might have been right after all.

She paused to listen again at the bedroom door. She didn't want to go in, in case she woke him. It was quiet, just the dozy sound of a fly butting against the window. It was warm upstairs; the sun had moved round to the back of the house. Mia pulled on a pair of shorts and a T-shirt and went downstairs to get a drink.

There was a bottle of white wine open in the fridge, left over from Dad's evening with Julie. The thin gold liquid in the clear bottle looked cool and inviting. Mia poured herself some, smiled as the wine glug-glugged into the glass. Delicious. She took it outside with her and lay on the grass in the sun. Above her, the swifts dipped and dived and screeched against the pale sky.

They'd had over two weeks of proper summery weather now. *Exam weather*, Dad called it. *It's always hot when the kids have exams*. Will and Becky and Tasha and everyone had the last one next week. Then they'd all be celebrating. Parties. Becky said she had to come. Her mum might babysit. Mia let her thoughts ramble as she sipped the wine.

She went back to get the bottle. Might as well top up her glass. Why shouldn't she enjoy herself? Everyone else was.

She looked at her watch. Nearly nine. She had an uneasy feeling somewhere in her stomach. Better check Kai. Then she'd have another glass. And cook herself something to eat, later. Dad and Julie would be settling down to salmon in filo pastry, baby potatoes, green beans. She could well imagine it. Dad would raise his full glass (Julie was driving): 'Cheers. Here's to us. And the end of term. Four weeks to go!'

Mia tiptoed into the bedroom. Kai had tried to kick his blanket off, but had merely wound himself tighter in it. His face was crimson, his cheeks tear-stained. She hadn't heard him. And the evening sun had been shining full on the back of the house, flooding the room with warmth and light. Through the gap she'd left in the drawn curtains, a strip of sun shone directly on to the Moses basket. Carefully, Mia loosened the blanket and folded it back, checked him. He was still fast asleep. Thank goodness. She pulled the curtains tighter together, to shade him. She thought of opening the window, but then the cat might get in. He could jump from the ash tree on to the windowsill if he was feeling energetic enough. He loved to sleep on Kai's basket.

Mia tiptoed out again. He'd be all right now. She'd check him again in a little while, just to make sure.

It was hard to settle outside now. The wine tasted slightly sour. She tipped the last glass down the sink.

Dad and Julie would be having dessert by now. Strawberry meringue with cream. Or a lemon sorbet, maybe, for Julie. Dad would be resisting the chocolate fudge cake to impress her. Two coffees.

Mia still wasn't hungry. She flipped the TV on, channel-hopped, switched off. Boring. She wandered outside again. The cat, Apple Pie, stalked over, tail high, and rubbed around her bare legs. Cupboard love. She gave him dry fish biscuits in his saucer near the back door. A slight breeze rattled the leaves of the ash tree. The bunches of seeds, keys, you called them, hung down like bright green party decorations. Colleen had made her look at them when she was here on Wednesday. Mia had told her how every autumn she and her sisters used to pick off sycamore keys on their way to school and pull open the little wings, balance them on their noses. They said they were unicorns. Colleen had laughed and tickled Kai and Zak's baby noses with the soft tip of an ash leaf.

She was full of it, Colleen. Of a sort of bubbling happiness. And of all the things they were going to do together. She talked as if Mia would always be here, in this house and garden; she couldn't imagine why she would ever want to be anywhere else.

Was that the cat miaowing? Mia listened. No, it was a baby's cry. It took a second to register. *Her* baby. Kai. Only it didn't sound like Kai's crying usually did. Mia shot inside and upstairs.

Kai lay with his eyes wide open, his face puce. He cried feebly, a bit like a newborn baby, or a kitten. She knew instantly that something was terribly wrong.

She snatched him up out of the basket. His hair was damp, his body hot and limp. Mia scrabbled with the poppers on the Babygro, trying to unfasten them. His vest underneath was damp and hot too, his skin red. His eyes looked weird, staring as if she wasn't there.

Her first impulse was to shake him out of it, to make him see her. But she knew that wasn't a good idea. What, then? He was much too hot. She must cool him down. She tried desperately to remember what Vicky had said about babies with temperatures. That was it. You sponged them down with a flannel. Warm water, not dead cold. She carried him into the bathroom.

Just as she was running the water in the basin, Kai's whole body started twitching horribly. Mia started to shake. He was going to die and it was her fault, and Dad's, too, because he had said leave him to cry and then he'd just gone out and left them both. What on earth should she do?

*Stop panicking. Think. Cool him down.* She sponged his face and body over and over, then she wrapped him in the towel and ran into Dad's room to use the phone. *Phone who?* In a panic, she could only think about Vicky. She'd know what to do. *Vicky's number? Where was it?* If she could find her mobile she had the number already programmed in. She ran downstairs, Kai bundled in her arms. He had gone quiet now. There. In her bag. She pressed the numbers.

'Slow down, I can't hear properly! Mia, is it?' Vicky's voice was calm. Mia instantly started to cry. She tried to explain what was happening.

'I'll come straight over. It'll take me ten minutes or so. If he has another fit, phone for an ambulance straight away. 999: emergency. Yes? Got that? He's got too hot, probably. Got a high temperature. Run a shallow lukewarm bath and lay him in it in your arms till he's cooled down a bit. Don't leave him. I'm coming right over.' She didn't sound so calm now. She made it seem really serious.

Mia rushed back into the bathroom with Kai and started to run the bath. If only she hadn't used up so much hot water before, for her own bath. It was barely lukewarm. It took so long. She sponged Kai's body with the flannel while she waited for the water to get deep enough. It felt much too cold. She knelt down beside the bath, laid Kai in the water, splashed the water over his tummy. He trembled. *Why was he so quiet?* Usually he'd kick his legs, splash with his hands, enjoy the water. *Hurry up, Vicky. Please.*

*Was he cooler now?* Mia thought so. *But might he not get too cold? That was dangerous, too.* She lifted Kai out of the bath and wrapped him loosely in the towel again. Then she found him a new nappy and a short-sleeved vest. He had started to whimper now, but his eyes still looked strange: empty and unfocused. Perhaps if she took him outside? While they waited for Vicky?

It seemed much longer than ten minutes. Finally Mia heard the sound of a car coming up Church Lane, the gear change as it came up the hill, and then the familiar red car drew up outside the gate. Vicky, in a short sundress instead of her usual grey uniform, ran into the garden.

'How is he? I came as quick as I could. Had to drop Sam off at my mum's on the way.' She fished her bag out of the car, got her thermometer out.

She took Kai from Mia, put her hand on his neck, on his head. 'He's still a bit hot, but not too bad now. We'll take his temperature and give him a proper check.'

Mia waited anxiously while Vicky put the thermometer under Kai's arm and felt his pulse.

'We might have to take him to Accident and Emergency in Ashton. Where's your dad?'

'Out. With his girlfriend.'

'Can you phone him?'

*Oh, no*, Mia thought. *Please no.*

'What is it?' Mia asked. 'What does it say?'

Vicky handed Kai back to her while she held the thermometer up. 'It's going down, by the look of things. But we'll need to keep an eye on him. It's really scary, I know, seeing your baby like that. It sounds like he had a fit – febrile convulsion, that's the proper name. And it's not that uncommon. It's when a baby gets too hot, and his temperature shoots up, and the fever sort of overwhelms him. So the main thing is to cool him down, quick. Which you did.'

Mia held Kai in her arms, rocked him, kissed his hot damp head over and over.

'We'll watch him, in case the fever was the start of something else, but it may have been the hot room, like you said. I'll ring the doctor, just in case, to put her on alert. See if there's anything else she recommends.' Vicky looked at Mia again. 'Hard being by yourself, though. Anyone would feel that. Really scary. What time's your dad back?'

Mia shrugged. 'He didn't say. I know where he is, though. I could phone him there.'

'Well, maybe we don't need to. I'll stay for a while, check Kai's all right. We'll phone him if we decide we need to go to the hospital. All right?'

That felt better. Perhaps Dad need never know. She didn't want him flapping around, fussing, finding fault.

Kai had settled down. His temperature had dropped down to nearly normal. There wasn't any danger of another fit now, Vicky said. They'd been lucky. But she'd stay a bit longer anyway.

'What about your little boy?' Mia asked.

'Sam can stay the night with my mother. He's used to it. I'll phone her, to check, in a minute. She likes to have him.'

'Sorry. To get you out.'

'It's all right, Mia. I'm pleased to help. But next time – well, hopefully there won't be a next time, but if there was, if he had another convulsion, don't take any risks. Not with a baby. Phone for an ambulance straight away.'

Vicky wasn't exactly cross, but Mia still felt told off.

'We need our support systems, us single mothers,' Vicky said. 'Having my mother round the corner makes all the difference. I couldn't manage without her. '

Mia didn't answer.

'It's too difficult otherwise.' She looked hard at Mia. 'How much are you on your own?'

Mia shook her head. 'It was just tonight. Please don't tell Dad.'

Vicky kept quiet. She looked thoughtful. Then, 'Do you want to make us a coffee or something? Not wine, unfortunately, because I'm driving.'

Had she noticed the glass and the empty bottle? Mia hoped not. She probably wouldn't mind, but Mia wasn't sure. Maybe she'd get totally the wrong idea about her. She might start thinking Mia wasn't coping very well. That she drank wine every evening or something. People did. It would be easy enough, alone all day. A cupboard full of bottles.

While Mia made coffee, Vicky carried Kai into the lounge and laid him in his Moses basket, lightly covered with a sheet.

'He's sleeping it off. That's normal. He'll probably sleep really well tonight.'

They left the French windows wide open, so they could listen out for him, and sat down on the lawn together.

'It's still beautifully warm. Perfect night for a party.'

'Why do you say that?'

'When I was driving here, I passed a whole crowd of young people. On their way to the beach, I imagine. Party time.'

Mia could feel her spine knotting, bone by bone, till her whole back was rigid. *Party time.* She knew who that must be. And they hadn't even invited her. Becky had promised! She'd made it sound like it would be later next week, after their last exam. Mia could have gone with Kai, couldn't she? Even if it was only for a little while. Gradually, they were forgetting all about her. It was too much.

The sobs just seemed to well up of their own accord. She'd thought Kai was going to die. Everyone was at a party and they hadn't even told her. And in any case, she couldn't have gone, because of Kai. It was all a huge horrible mess.

Vicky didn't say much. She let Mia cry for ages, and then she put her arm round her and hugged her tight. Eventually, they drank their cold coffees. It was beginning to get dark.

'Do you want me to stay till your dad gets back?'

'No!' Mia said. 'I mean, there's no need. As long as you're sure Kai's going to be all right.'

'We'll have one last look. And I'll take his temperature again. And you can always phone. I'll leave my mobile on. Or there's the hospital. Yes?'

'You're not even on duty,' Mia said.

'Well, I'd only do it for you!' Vicky smiled.

'And Colleen.'

'Well, maybe Colleen, too. I've got time for you two. Like you both. And the babies. And I know what it's like. Remember? I've been there, too.'

Mia remembered. Vicky had had Sam when she was only seventeen. But she'd got on fine. Got herself together. It was possible, even for a teenage mum.

'I'm glad you and Colleen are getting on,' Vicky said. 'I thought you'd like each other.'

'She's been over here loads of times now,' Mia said. 'She loves the garden. And the sea.'

'Well, it must be wonderful compared to that flat she's living in at the moment. It was all we could find, at short notice. It's not for long, though. She's used to being outside, what with travelling and the fair. And this is a lovely garden. You're really lucky.'

Mia didn't answer. She was fed up with people telling her how lucky she was. She didn't feel lucky at all.

'Anyway,' Vicky went on, 'Colleen's mum will be able to have her back soon, now she's so much better. She's got one more appointment to go, I think. And hopefully Isaac's putting on weight now.'

That was another thing. If Colleen left, went back with the fair, where would that leave Mia? She'd have nobody soon.

When Vicky had driven off, Mia carried Kai in his basket upstairs to the bedroom. He was getting heavier. She needed both hands and had to stop halfway up for a breather. She put the basket down by the bed, stroked his cheek. He was sleeping soundly now. She kissed his cheek tenderly. Her precious baby.

'*Night-night, sleep tight. Sweet dreams.*' That was Mum's voice, suddenly coming back to her over the years. What she used to say as she tiptoed out of Mia's bedroom. Funny, the way it had just popped into her head.

Mia pulled the curtains back, opened the window wide and looked out into the night. As if on cue, a huge full moon was rising, silver and mysterious. It would be so beautiful, watching that moon rise over the sea. Mia wasn't sure whether she was imagining it, or whether she could actually hear laughter and voices drifting up the hill from the party on the shore.

## CHAPTER FIFTEEN

Mia woke up briefly in the night. She lay listening in the darkness, wondering what had woken her. Kai was sleeping soundly. She put her hand on his head: cool, no temperature. Thank God for that. She reached out for the clock: just after midnight. Strange, it felt like she'd been asleep for much longer than an hour or so. Then she heard voices, low, and the bathroom door creaked. Dad and Julie. She must be staying the night. That meant she'd be there first thing, having breakfast, and would probably be staying around all day, since it was Saturday. There was no way Mia was going to be around for that.

She woke again with Kai at five thirty. She fed him in the bed, both of them still sleepy, and they dozed together like that till after six. It would be another beautiful day. The sun was already up, the sky a clear blue.

A new day. A new start.

Mia got dressed, leaving Kai on the bed, bolstered

in with pillows so he couldn't slip off. She went into her sister Kate's room, opened the wardrobe doors and rifled through the dresses and skirts she'd left hanging there, all the clothes she couldn't fit into her backpack. The dress Mia had borrowed last summer, the one she'd been wearing that first time she and Will made love in the field by the beach, was hanging there. On an impulse, Mia took it off the hanger and slipped it on. It still fitted, more or less. Just a bit tight at the top, where it had hung loose before. She smoothed the silky fabric over her thighs. If Colleen could wear a silk dress on the beach, why shouldn't she?

She rummaged through the chest of drawers in her own room to find something nice for Kai. Becky's Babygro with the sea horses. It was still a bit big, but that didn't matter. And it would still be cool outside, so she found him a little knitted cardigan with fish-shaped buttons, a present from Annie.

She went downstairs quietly. No one else awake. Good. Dad's door was tight shut.

Mia put Kai into the buggy and strapped him in. She twirled the plastic stars and fishes on elastic which she'd stretched across the front of the buggy to keep him happy. In the kitchen, she found a length of French bread and some cheese, and then she plucked two ripe peaches from the fruit bowl on the table.

She filled a plastic bottle with cold water from the jug in the fridge. All that could go in the changing bag on the rack under the buggy. There. Almost ready. It still wasn't even half past six.

She looked around. What else? She picked up the rug she and Colleen put on the grass for the babies sometimes and folded it ready. On the hall table she noticed two paperback books: new, by the look of them. She shoved them in the bag, too. You never knew, she might feel like reading, if Kai went to sleep. It was something to do, wasn't it? They probably belonged to Miss English Teacher Blackman but so what? She shouldn't have left them there if she wanted them.

Mia unbolted the front door and pushed Kai's buggy over the threshold.

The garden was full of birdsong. The blackbird she recognized, singing from the top of the ash tree, but there were thousands of others, it seemed, in the garden and all the trees around. There was a nest high in the ivy on the wall. The cat, Apple Pie, skulked along the path underneath, watching and waiting. Mia shooed him away.

The grass was still damp with dew and the buggy left silvery wheel tracks. Mia smiled at Kai.

'We're going down to the sea, you and me!' she said.

The lane was quiet. No one else seemed to be around. For this moment, the world belonged to her and Kai. It felt good to be up so early, pushing out with a sense of purpose. They branched off on to the footpath, still lined with fading cow parsley and elderflower. Mia picked a fistful of little white flowers like stars and tucked them into the elastic alongside the plastic fish for Kai to look at. They went past the field, her and Will's field, and she showed it to Kai. 'Here's where you began,' she told him. The swallows were there still, or maybe the fledglings of the swallows that had been there last summer, dipping and diving with a flash of white on blue and their fine forked tails.

'Swallows!' she showed Kai.

His eyes were bright this morning, she thought. Clearer and brighter than before. They emerged from the tunnel of overhanging trees on to the rough strip of land above the pebbly beach. The brightness of sunshine on water was dazzling for a minute. Mia reached forwards and pulled Kai's hat down to shade his eyes.

'There you are! The sea!'

She turned the buggy round to face the water. Kai's eyes crinkled up in the light.

A cool breeze ruffled Mia's dress and she shivered slightly. They'd have to find somewhere out of the wind and that meant pushing the buggy over the stones. Kai seemed to hate that, but it was such hard work carrying him. Still, there was no hurry. She could carry him first, maybe, leave him safely propped up, and then go back for the buggy.

She unstrapped Kai and lifted him out. His head didn't wobble so much now and his warm little body curled in towards her, knowing her shape. He stretched out one little hand, a starfish. She smiled at him, and for a second his face quivered, his mouth moved into something very like a smile. Mia felt tears pricking her eyes. Just because he smiled! She was getting as daft as Colleen.

Mia picked her way over the stones, pulling the buggy behind her with one hand. The other supported Kai. She went westwards, away from Whitecross and Stonegate. It was all right for a bit, but her arm began to ache and so she abandoned the buggy and went on with just Kai. Her lips brushed the top of his head and she murmured to him as they walked. Something like a tune came, though she did not know the words that went with it. Colleen was always singing to Isaac.

Round the next bend Mia saw the spot she'd been making for. The beach curved round, and there was an outcrop of larger boulders which you could lean up against and which offered some shelter. As they got closer she could see the remains of a fire: half-burnt driftwood, a circle of grey ash, a stack of empty bottles and cans half-buried in the gritty sand. So this was where they'd had the party. She'd suspected as much.

Mia kicked the ash with her toe and watched the flakes whirl up and settle again. Seeing the fire made her hurt inside all over again. But Kai's fist caught hold of her hair at that moment; he pulled. And as he did so, he smiled again. It was a real smile, she was sure now.

'You!' she said. She kissed his hand and untangled her hair. 'We might as well stop here,' she told him.

She pulled one of the unburnt tree branches closer so she could sit on it and lean against the rocks. The beach was damp, even though the tide didn't come up this far. She rested Kai on her lap, leaning against her chest, facing out. They dozed in the early-morning sun.

Crunching. Boots on pebbles. Coming closer. Mia opened her eyes. Kai still slept, his head lolled against her, his hat flopped over his face. Mia felt annoyed that there should be anyone else on the beach this early in the day. Somebody from Whitecross, walking a dog probably. She screwed her eyes up: the figure was a dark silhouette against the bright sunshine.

Of course. Who else? This perfect morning, it had to be him, didn't it? He must have been up all night, stayed on the beach after the party when everyone else had gone home. He'd seen her, stopped. Considered. Started walking again. Perhaps he'd just walk straight past. But no, he stopped just before he got to her.

'Hi, Mia,' he said.

'Hello.'

'You're out early.'

'So are you.'

'Well. Yeah. Been out all night.'

'Good party, was it?' Mia hoped she sounded suitably sarcastic. There was a slight pause.

'It was OK.'

'That's all right, then.'

He looked at her sheepishly. 'I thought Becky would've invited you.'

'No.'

'I suppose, well, everyone thought you'd, well, not be able to come.'

'Suppose.'

'Would you?'

'Would I what?'

'Have come?'

'Probably not.'

'You didn't miss much.'

'I would have liked the fire.'

'Yes. You always did, didn't you?'

There was a silence, filled only by the wash of water against stone.

'Tide's coming up,' Will said.

'It doesn't come this far, though,' Mia said. 'We'll be OK.' She knew he was confused by the 'we'. 'Me and Kai,' she said, to explain.

'Can I sit down?'

'If you want.'

'Tell you what, I'll make you a fire now,' Will said. 'Seeing as you missed it last night.'

Mia smiled.

'Shall I?'

'If you want.'

She watched him while he sorted the half-burnt logs, searched along the tideline for other pieces of driftwood, snapped dry grass for tinder. He didn't have matches, but he had his old flint-striker in his jeans pocket. Of course. Eventually he got a tiny flame to spurt and catch the dry grass and bark.

He sat back next to her on the log. For the first time, he looked at Kai. She could see an embarrassed flush run along his neck, up over his face.

'How is he?' Will asked, shy.

'Kai's doing well,' Mia said. 'Except for last night, when I thought he was going to die.'

Will looked at her sharply. 'What do you mean?'

She told him what had happened. Why shouldn't he know the details? About all the things she was having to deal with? While he was having a good time with all her friends at a party.

'I don't know what to say,' Will said when she'd finished.

Mia shrugged. 'Not a lot you can say.'

'Well, I'm sorry. And I'm glad he's OK.'

'Are you?' Mia looked directly into Will's eyes.

He blushed. 'Yes. Of course.'

'There's no *of course* about it!' Mia snapped. 'If he'd died it might have been easier for everyone.'

'Don't say that. Not now,' Will said. 'You don't mean it, do you?'

There was a pause, while Mia thought how to answer him.

She spoke truthfully. 'No. It's really hard and everything, but I love him now, my little Kai.'

She still couldn't read the expression on Will's face. Embarrassment mixed with something else.

Will fed more sticks on to the fire. 'Should've brought some bacon or something. For breakfast.'

'I'm not hungry,' Mia said.

'I am. Shall I go and get us some? When the garage opens at Whitecross?'

'That won't be for ages. Have some of my bread if you want. Or a peach. I left my bag on the buggy.'

'I saw it when I came along the beach. Shall I get it for you?'

'Or you could hold him while I fetch it.' Mia shifted Kai up a little.

'It's OK. I'll get the buggy.'

Mia smiled wryly. *He doesn't want to hold him*, she realized, *because he's scared*.

It was bizarre to see him pulling a baby buggy along the beach. Good thing there wasn't anyone else to see; he'd never have lived it down if Matt or Liam had been there.

Kai was awake now. He blinked in the sunlight, gave a tiny sneeze.

'That's your daddy!' she whispered in his little shell ear. Words came into her head from way back. *Dance for your daddy, my little laddie*. Something about a boat and a fish.

She watched Will's bumpy progress along the shingle. The bag kept slipping off and he had to refold the rug. In the end he dumped both inside the buggy and carried it like that.

'It's heavy!' he said. 'Wouldn't you be better off with that sling thing that Mum gave you?'

'I lost it.'

'I saw you,' Will said, 'the other day. Wednesday? With another girl.'

'That's my new friend, Colleen,' Mia said. 'She's got a baby, too.'

'I saw.'

'Where were you, then? We didn't see you. Why didn't you come over?'

Will shrugged. 'Didn't know if you'd want me to. You were mucking about in the water. Crazy! You were both soaked through.'

He shoved another log into the fire. He didn't need to, but it was something to do. The wood was burning well now, cleanly, without much smoke. Mia leaned back, to keep Kai safely out of the sparks that every so often flared and spun upwards like fireflies.

Will scuffed about the beach, searching out flat pebbles for skimming.

'Did you know,' he said, 'that there's no such thing as a completely round pebble?'

'Who says?' Mia teased.

'It's a fact. Honest.'

'I'll prove you wrong, then.'

Mia leaned over Kai, scrabbling among the pebbles she could reach from where she was sitting. They were all shapes and colours, no two the same. Lots of egg-shaped ones, but none were perfectly round.

'Here. You hold him while I look.'

She held Kai out. He didn't have a choice. She saw him waver, ready to refuse, but she suddenly knew he wouldn't.

'You have to support his head still,' Mia said. She carefully put Kai into his arms and he sat down, the baby stiff and awkward on his lap. Mia laughed. 'I don't know who's more scared, you or him.'

Will tried to laugh, but his voice came out funny.

'You're all right,' Mia said. 'There's no one looking. No one else here but us.'

'It's not that,' Will said.

'What, then?'

'It feels – I don't know what. I can't believe it. That he's such a – that he's real. A little person. Like me or you.'

Mia walked a little way along the beach, hunting out pebbles. She could sense them both watching her, willing her not to go too far. Kai began to whimper and Will called to her. She couldn't resist it, that brief moment of power; she walked just a little further, until Kai started to cry properly, and then she turned back.

'Babies always cry when I hold them,' Will said, gingerly handing Kai back as if he were explosive material.

'And which babies would this be?'

'You know, at Tasha's or whatever.'

'Once, maybe.'

'Well, you know what I mean. I'm not very good with them.'

'He doesn't know you, that's all.'

*Not yet*, she wanted to add, but she didn't. Instead she found herself asking about Ali. The words just blurted out.

'So are you going out with Ali?'

'Who told you that?'

'I heard about the party. Ali's party. You must have known I would.'

'That. Yes, well, I drank too much. I was upset.'

'*You* were upset? I'd just had Kai. Couldn't you think for one second what it might be like for *me*?'

Mia was trembling all over. Kai started to cry. Now it was all going to go wrong again, like last time. She stood up, took a deep breath, jiggled Kai against her shoulder, shushed him.

'Anyway,' Will said. 'I'm not going out with her. Since you asked.'

He sat, silent, poking a stick into the fire, stirring up the embers into red-hot sparks. Mia turned half away and stared at the sea. She held Kai against her shoulder, his eyes peeping over it at the sparks.

'I'm sorry,' he finally said. 'I've made a mess of everything. But we weren't together, were we, for months before – before Ali's party. So I don't understand, really . . .' His voice trailed slightly. 'I'm going away soon, anyway.'

Mia turned back to face him. 'Where?'

'Not far. It's just a holiday job, for the summer. The camping and caravan place at Mill Cove. I can live up there. I get my own caravan for the summer.'

Mia shifted Kai to the other shoulder.

'He needs a feed,' she said.

'I'll go,' Will said.

'You don't have to.'

'No, I'll go and get bacon and stuff. For breakfast. You might be hungry by then. Don't worry about the fire. I can get it going again when I come back.'

*Maybe it isn't going so badly wrong after all*, Mia thought, as she unbuttoned the top of her dress so she could feed Kai. He'd wanted to sit with her. Had made the fire for her. Had even held Kai. Said he wasn't going out with Ali. So what if he was working away for the summer? Perhaps she might even go and visit him in the caravan. They could just turn up, her and Kai. If there was a bus that went near. She felt cheered up about Ali. He'd gone to get the bacon and was coming back. All good signs.

He'd held Kai for the very first time. Said sorry.

She was glad she was wearing the dress. She knew it suited her. Wondered whether he remembered it, from last summer. She hadn't meant to get so cross with him, but that was how it always was with her. He knew that.

Mia imagined describing the conversation to Colleen. She'd laugh. She'd probably say something like, 'Why don't you just come straight out and tell him you still like him? Why mess about? Then he can say yes or no.'

Colleen didn't really understand how complicated it was. And the truth was, she, Mia, didn't really know what she wanted from Will. Did she really think they could go out together, as if Kai didn't exist? What did they have in common anyway? He'd be starting A levels in September, and then going off to university. He was getting his music together now, playing gigs at pubs even, Becky said. While she was doing what exactly? Looking after a baby.

The sun felt warm on her back and shoulders. It drew out the smells of the beach, a mixture of rotting seaweed and salt and something else, the accumulated stink of all the rubbish washed up by each tide. Not far away she could see a rotten stump of wood that looked like a dead dog. It could be, almost. Nothing would surprise her. Sometimes there were bits of clothing, or a waterlogged trainer, or old condoms and tampons flushed out of the sewage outlet further up the coast. You'd probably catch something if you swam in the sea here. You had to go right up the coast if you wanted to swim. Dad used to take them in the car. They hadn't done that for years.

She was thirsty. She reached out for the bag and pulled out the bottle of water. Still only eight forty-five. Dad and Julie probably weren't even up yet. She had hours to kill. She wondered what Colleen was doing today. Colleen didn't have a phone, so Mia would have to wait for her to call from a phone box.

Kai was sleepy after his feed. Mia arranged the buggy so he could have some shade and put him in it. She covered him loosely with a blanket, rocked the buggy to and fro until he was properly asleep.

The fire was almost out. She collected up more dry grass and small sticks and fed them into the glowing embers. Little by little she coaxed the fire back into life. You didn't need big flames for cooking, just the white heat of logs that have been burning for a while.

Will seemed to take ages. Perhaps he wasn't coming back after all.

She finally saw the distant figure trudging along the shore from Whitecross, a plastic bag swinging from one hand.

'Had to wait for it to open,' he explained.

He opened the packet of bacon with the blade of his penknife. Then he chose sticks to whittle into a point, peeled back the bark, speared rolls of raw bacon on to each, ready for cooking.

'I got bread, too.'

She was hungry now. The bacon tasted better than usual, cooked like this on an open fire. Will sat next to her on the log, his thigh almost touching hers.

'What were the exams like?' Mia asked.

'OK. Not bad, really. I should be OK for next year.'

'There was never any doubt about that.'

'Try telling my mum that.'

'She's stupid, then. You've been top all year in almost everything. You could have done anything you liked next year. They were falling over you, the teachers, trying to get you to do their subject.'

'Don't exaggerate.'

'I'm not. Miss Blackman was heartbroken when you didn't choose A level English. And that history teacher.'

Will laughed.

'When are you off, then?' Mia asked.

'Middle of July. For six weeks.'

'Becks says you've been playing in a band,' Mia said.

'Yeah. It's good. We've started writing our own stuff. But we need a fiddle player. Don't know anyone, do you?'

'Hardly. I don't see anyone any more.'

'It won't be like that for long, though.'

'No?'

'What do you think you'll do? Will you do retakes?'

'Hardly retakes. I haven't done them the first time, have I?'

'Well, you've done some of the coursework.'

'Hardly any.'

'Becky's going to college for her As. You could go there.'

'With Kai?'

'Well, there's crèches and things. Mum found out about it for you.'

'I don't want to talk about it.'

They finished eating in silence.

'I'm going up to Mill Cove later this morning,' Will said, 'to see someone about that job.'

Mia picked up a stone, aimed it at one of the sunken beer bottles. Missed. Will aimed, hit it first time. Mia's eyes prickled with hot tears. Nothing was fair.

'Do you want to come?' he asked her.

'How can I?'

'My brother's giving me a lift. You could put the buggy in the back. Or we could leave it back at the house.'

'How will you get back?'

'Hitch a lift, probably.'

She hesitated. It was tempting. She had Kai's bag of stuff, after all. Maybe she and Kai could get a bus back or something. It was better than staying all day on this stinking beach by herself. Or going home to Dad and Julie.

'All right,' she said.

'We can pick you up at the end of the lane if you want. Then we won't have to see Mum or anyone. Ben won't mind.'

'What about the people at the caravan park?'

'You can wait outside, or go down to the cove, to the cafe there, while I'm seeing them. Give me three-quarters of an hour.'

'OK.'

Mia watched him go. Then she watched the sea for a bit. The tide was almost at high-water mark. The small waves crept in, broke, spread out like lace table-cloths on the gritty sand. Every so often a bigger wave came further in.

A tiny bubble of happiness floated inside her. She willed it to last. Like watching a soap bubble you'd blown though one of those little plastic hoops when you were little, and sometimes you blew a perfect one, rainbow-coloured, and you watched it take off, up, over the wall, over the hedge, up into the sky until you couldn't see it any more. And you imagined that fragile little bubble floating on and on, out into the blue.

Briefly she thought of Dad. He would have no idea where she was. Still, that was his lookout. She was sixteen, wasn't she? She didn't have to have his permission for a day out. He had Julie now, anyway. They could have the day by themselves for once.

The fire had died right down. She packed her stuff together, looked at her watch. It would take her at least ten minutes to get the buggy along the beach and up on to the lane. The sun was rising higher, the shadows already shortening. And she had a whole day ahead with Will.

## CHAPTER SIXTEEN

'Thanks, Ben.' Will slammed the car door.

'OK, Daddy-boy! Any time!' Ben grinned, pulled out and off down the road before Will could register what his brother had said.

'Sorry. He's a pain.' Will grimaced. 'Can't wait till I can drive, then I won't need lifts from him. Only four months to go.'

Nothing was going to spoil Mia's mood. She was out with Will, and it was sunny and hot, and just down the road was a beautiful sandy cove. There was even a cafe. It was like being on holiday.

'I'll see you at the cafe, shall I? My meeting won't take long.'

Mia could understand now why families came to places like this. It was easy with a baby. You could park a car right near the beach for one thing, instead of walking for miles. The campsite had play equipment for children, and millions of notices about slowing down for pedestrians, and clean toilet blocks and places where you could wash up and get water. There was even a baby-changing place with free wipes and a comfy chair for nursing mothers.

*How sad am I?* she thought. *I sound like Mel from the young mums group.* She was glad she hadn't said anything like that to Will.

The holiday season hadn't got going properly yet and the cafe wasn't crowded. Mia parked the buggy at a table outside, overlooking the cove, and went in to order herself a drink. She watched a family at another table for a while, then the girls serving at the bar. Her sort of age. She could imagine doing a Saturday job somewhere like this. Perhaps she could even bring Kai. There was a small girl with fair curly hair bobbing in and out of the tables, getting under the waitresses' feet. Every so often one of the girls said something to her. An older woman handed her a lolly. She seemed to belong there in the cafe, although Mia couldn't work out which of the girls was her mother. They all seemed to share her.

Mia rummaged in her bag for something to do and found the paperback books. She read the blurbs on the back, chose the one with the best cover, started to read.

'Good, is it?'

Will, sun on his golden hair, stood before her. He

smiled. *Those eyes! Like the sea.* She imagined every-one watching them. The waitresses, the girls at the bar. Fancying him.

'Yes, actually. Don't look so surprised. I can still read a book, you know.'

'Don't remember you ever reading one before,' he teased.

'Do you want to stay here?'

'Let's have a drink, then go down on the beach.'

He ordered two bottles of beer. No one asked how old he was.

It made her feel light-headed. She thought of the wine she'd had the night before. Better check that Kai wasn't getting too hot. She felt the back of his neck, as Vicky had shown her. Fine.

'So how did your meeting go?'

'Cool. I've definitely got the job. It's shifts, that's why you get to live in a caravan. I might have to share it, though, with some of the other temporary workers.'

That was disappointing. So much for her fantasy about her and Kai coming to visit, staying a while.

When they'd finished their drinks they went down the slope to the beach. She carried Kai while Will brought the buggy. So much easier with two of them. They went right along to the far side of the cove, where there weren't any other people and there was some shade for Kai. Mia spread the rug out. When she kicked off her shoes and wriggled herself straight on the rug, Will touched her hair.

It was starting all over again.

Will pulled his T-shirt over his head and lay next to her in his rolled-up jeans. His leg touched hers. He stroked one finger the length of her arm, made the flesh shiver. 'You look much better,' he said.

'Than what?'

'Than before. You know. When I last saw you. You look like you again.'

She wished she felt like the old her. He had no idea, did he, what had happened to her? How completely changed she was, forever, by having a baby. None of it showed on the outside.

'I might swim later,' he said.

'I haven't got swimming things.'

'Nor have I. I'll go naked.'

'Will, you can't. Not here! There's people around.'

He laughed. 'In just boxers, then. If you insist.'

'*I* don't mind.'

'Why don't you take his things off? Let him kick about? Babies can go naked!'

Mia hadn't thought of that. It was a good idea. She undid his Babygro and then unfastened the nappy so he could lie on it, bare-bottomed. Kai kicked his legs enthusiastically.

'See. He likes that,' Will said.

195

They both laughed as a golden arc of pee landed on Will's arm.

'What do you expect?' Mia smiled. She looked down at Kai tenderly. 'He's smiling. It's his new thing,' she told Will. 'New today.'

'He's got a good aim,' Will said. 'Like me.'

What did he mean? Was he acknowledging some sort of connection between them, father and son? *Too soon for that*, Mia thought. *Don't rush it. Enjoy this moment. Don't think about everything so much.*

And for a while it was completely perfect, her and Will, and Kai, lying together on the rug in warm June sunshine, the sea a sparkling turquoise, lapping at the sand. Every time Will touched her, even by accident, his body so close to hers on the rug, she felt her flesh fizz with excitement. She'd give anything to be alone with him now.

But she wasn't.

Kai got bored first. It was too bright, too hot, too still for him. He started to grizzle, and then Will got fidgety. He didn't like sunbathing anyway, he said. He'd go for a swim. Mia tried to feed Kai while he was gone, but there seemed to be sand everywhere, and he kept turning his head away from her breast, not concentrating properly, and milk from her other breast started leaking on to the dress in an embarrassing dark patch.

Mia felt suddenly hot and cross. Will was taking ages; she couldn't see him even. He must have walked round the rocks into the tiny cove the other side, and there was no way Mia could get round there with Kai. She started packing up their things, folded the rug, strapped Kai into the buggy to keep him off the sand, and that made him wail. Still Will didn't come.

She waited for ages. Kai was miserable. She had to get off the hot beach soon; she couldn't risk him getting a temperature again.

Mia started to panic. Where was Will? Who did he think he was, just going off like that? It was just so typical of him. Just thinking about himself, what he wanted to do. Probably looking at some fascinating rock formation or an unusual species of seabird half-way up the cliff. With not a thought for her, or Kai. Why did he have to spoil everything? She'd give him till two and then she'd just go.

It got to two, and then quarter past. Half past. Right. That was it. He'd said he was just going for a swim and instead he'd wandered off for over an hour.

Mia dragged the buggy across the sand. It clogged up the wheels. Kai sobbed. A family making their way to the toilets took pity on her and the man gave her a hand. They carried the buggy between them as far as the concrete slope.

'It's hard work by yourself!' the man said cheerily.

As if she hadn't noticed. The woman gave a weary smile. 'Babies and beaches. They don't mix. Better when he's bigger.'

Mia was ready to cry. She was miles from home, alone with a baby. Will didn't care about anyone but himself. How could he be so thoughtless? And how was she going to get back? She'd only ever come here by car. Perhaps someone at the campsite would know about buses. If there was one. And she could change Kai in the toilets there, get some of the sand off him.

The man at the campsite reception got out a bundle of timetables from a drawer and tried to be helpful. Two a day on a Saturday went to Ashton bus station. She'd missed the first. The other one was at five thirty. The stop was down the lane a bit. No seat or shelter. She'd do better to wait at the cafe.

'Thanks,' Mia said bitterly.

That was where Will found her.

'Mia! There you are! You could have said! I've been looking everywhere.'

'*You* have? I waited *hours* for you! You said you were going for a swim but you just disappeared for hours!'

'I only walked round the rocks a bit, to the next cove. Why didn't you come and look for me if you were worried?'

'I wasn't worried about you!' Mia was spitting with rage. 'I was worried about Kai. He was much too hot and miserable on the beach. I told you he'd had a temperature last night. You could have thought! But no, that's impossible, isn't it? You can't think of any-one but yourself.'

Her head ached. Her words echoed round and round her skull. She knew them so well: they came straight out of her own father's mouth. Stones dropped carelessly into a still pond, making ripples that spread into ever-widening circles.

She'd blown it now. Will wouldn't want anything more to do with her. Or Kai.

A young waitress with her notepad flipped over ready came up to Mia's table and hovered, trying to catch Will's eye. 'Can I get you anything?' she asked anxiously.

'No. We're just going!' Mia snapped.

'Thanks. Sorry.' Will smiled apologetically at the girl.

'You're so nice to everyone else!' Mia hissed. There was no stopping her now. 'But they don't know the real you, do they? How selfish and scared and spineless you really are. Well, we're better off without you, me and Kai.'

Everyone at the cafe was watching now. Will's face was scarlet. He tried to grab the handle of the buggy.

'Cool it, Mia. You can't just storm off here. How do you think you're going to get home?'

'What do you care? I'll hitch a lift.'

'No way, Mia. It's not safe!'

'You'd do it!'

'But that's different!'

'Why? Because you're a bloke?'

'Well, yes – and look at you – you're in a real state – you can't go off like this. Please, Mia. Wait a minute.'

She was already pushing up the lane. Her head throbbed. She was hot all over. She knew she was being stupid, but she didn't know what else to do. It was over an hour till the bus was due, and then it would take over an hour to get to Ashton, by which time she'd have missed the bus to Whitecross.

She slowed down. She'd half expected Will to come running after her. She hesitated, listened for footsteps, looked back. He was walking up the lane, carrying two ice creams. He held one out to her. As if that would make everything all right! *Just like Dad might have*, Mia thought, *when I was a little girl*.

'I'm sorry,' he said, catching her up. 'I didn't think. You're completely right. I've no idea what it's like with a baby.'

The apology completely disarmed her. She took the

ice cream, started licking the drips round the edge of the cone.

'Look,' Will said, 'let me phone Ben. He'll come and get us. Give us a lift back. I know he's insufferable, but at least he's got a car.'

'OK,' Mia said.

'Let's find a shady place to sit. Why don't I show you the caravan that'll be mine? Then we'll find somewhere to wait for Ben.'

Mia, Will, Kai. They looked like a proper family, pushing the buggy over the field to the small white caravan next to the hedge. They might be going home.

*Wake up, Mia. Get real!* She kept on doing it, drifting into this romantic dream where everything turned out all right: Will and her deeply in love, setting up home together somewhere – the fantasy didn't quite stretch to the details, like money, and houses, and jobs – and it all being exciting and fun, with lots of other friends dropping in, and her discovering she had this amazing talent which had somehow never shown up at school.

But it wasn't going to be like that, was it? Why couldn't she get it?

Mia sat in the back of the car with Kai, and Will sat next to his brother at the front, fiddling with the radio. From time to time Ben asked Mia a question. He sounded as if he were laughing. In the end she closed her eyes and pretended to sleep.

He stopped the car in Church Lane and helped her get the buggy out of the boot.

'Thanks, Ben.'

Will stayed inside the car.

'See ya!'

Ben drove off. She hadn't said goodbye to Will, nor he to her.

It was a shock to see Vicky's car in the drive, and Dad and Julie and Vicky standing round in a circle, deep in conversation.

They all looked up as she pushed the buggy round into the garden. Dad's face was like thunder.

'Where the hell have you been?'

Vicky stepped forwards, put her hand on Dad's arm. 'It's all right. They're safe, that's the main thing.'

Mia stared, bewildered. As if enough hadn't happened already today.

Vicky's face was serious. 'Mia, your Dad's been very worried and upset. We didn't know where you were – couldn't find you anywhere – no one knew.'

Mia sighed.

Vicky went on, 'I probably made things worse. I

phoned to check how Kai was this morning, and then, when we realized you weren't at home – well, we all panicked a bit.'

Mia leaned over the buggy, unstrapped Kai and picked him up. Playing for time. Waiting for the next onslaught.

'I'll put the kettle on,' Julie said brightly. 'Who'd like tea?'

No one answered her. She disappeared anyway into the kitchen.

Mia scowled.

Dad was gearing up for the next round. 'Did it not occur to you, Mia, that we might be a little concerned about you? Leaving the house at some God-early hour, no note, no brief phone call even to let us know. Funny, I should be used to it by now. But I keep expecting that you will grow up. Learn a little consideration. Think beyond your own goldfish bowl.'

More stones. Bigger ripples.

She'd forgotten all about her mobile. Hadn't even taken it with her.

She was so tired. The early start, the beach, the long, hot drive home, the walk up the hill. All she wanted was a long cold drink, and a lie-down, and for everyone to go away and leave her alone. Including Kai.

'You take him, then, if you're so concerned. I've

had enough.' She thrust the baby at Dad, pushed past Vicky, ran upstairs and shut the bedroom door. She lay on the bed, heart thumping.

They left her for a while. Low voices drifted up from outside the window. Dad was still going on and on. Fragments of sentences reached her. *Enough ... That's it ... mother will have to ...* Vicky's tones were soothing, calming him down, reasoning.

Footsteps came up the stairs and there was a light knock at the door. Vicky opened it.

'Mia? Can I come in?'

She came in anyway.

'Kai's with your dad. He's fine.'

'I know.'

'I'm sorry if I've made things worse. I just called to check how Kai was this morning, and spoke to your dad, so I had to explain what had happened, I'm afraid, and then of course he got in a panic when he couldn't find you. He phoned Becky and some of your other friends, and no one knew anything, so then he phoned me back and I thought of Colleen, so I offered to go and see her, since she's not on the phone ... You can see how complicated it got. We even phoned the hospital.'

Mia groaned.

'I know. We probably overreacted. Still, it shows we all care about you very much. And Kai.' Vicky spoke gently but insistently. 'So what happened? Where were you?'

'Out.'

'Mia, please cooperate. There is an issue here. I'm trying to help.'

'I got up early, and I didn't want to be here with Dad's girlfriend, and so I went down to the beach. OK? And I looked after Kai really carefully. I've made sure he's not got too hot. So you can't get me on that.'

'I'm not trying to *get* you. Don't be ridiculous. Look. You're obviously tired. Have a rest and I'll talk to you and your dad at a better time. Monday morning, yes? I'll come to you first thing before my other visits.'

'OK.'

She listened to Vicky's car driving away, and then there were more voices, and the sound of another car, and she knew Julie had gone, too. So that left Dad and Kai. Waiting for her to come downstairs.

*Let them wait.*

They talked over supper. Dad had cooked a chicken. He'd even bought strawberries for pudding, expecting Julie to be there. Mia and he ate the meal instead, watched by Kai from his bouncy chair.

'It's been a horrible day,' Dad said. 'I'm sorry I lost

it with you. I've been trying really hard, you know, recently, to make allowances. But this was one step too far. You realize Julie left, don't you, because of you? That's not fair, is it? I know you don't approve, but I'm entitled to my life, and it's going to include her, one way or another.'

'What do you mean?'

'We'd like to live together sometime. In the autumn maybe, when she's sold her place. Or she might rent it out for a while, till we're sure. It's early days; we've only just started talking about it. But I don't want your behaviour spoiling my chance of happiness.'

*His chance of happiness. What about hers? Who was thinking about that? No one. Not even her.*

'We have to make some plans, Mia. We can't go on like this.'

'No.'

'Well? I know you hate talking about the future, but we have to.'

She felt her face harden, a mask.

'So?'

'What?'

'What had you thought? Any idea, beyond staying here and looking after Kai and seeing your friends?'

'You make it sound like none of that's important.'

'No, I'm trying to be realistic. I know babies are

206

a full-time job. But they also have to be supported financially. And a sixteen-year-old girl needs something more, too. Isn't that right? I wondered about your mother –'

'No.' Mia flushed. 'No way.'

'You haven't heard me out yet. If you lived with her you could go to that school for teenage mums. They look after the babies while you study. Get some exams under your belt. And you can claim benefits if you're in full-time education, and it would give me a bit of a breathing space.'

'She doesn't want me, Dad. It wouldn't work out, you know that. She's got Bryan and now you've got Julie and nobody cares for me at all.' Her voice finished on a high-pitched whine.

She knew she sounded pathetic.

'What do you suggest, then?'

'I don't know. I'm not ready. It's still too soon. Kai's only six weeks old. I'm sorry about today, but please, Dad, give me a bit of space. I'll think about it, I will, I promise.'

He didn't believe her, she could tell. He noisily cleared the plates away and went out into the garden, started pulling up weeds savagely.

Kai watched Mia anxiously as she moved about the kitchen, putting things away, wiping the surfaces. His eyes were like bright buttons.

'It's all right, Birdy,' she told him. 'We'll be all right, won't we?'

She took Kai to bed with her early. Dad was on the phone when she came out of the bathroom, talking softly so she couldn't hear.

She lay awake in the too-light bedroom. Kai nestled beside her in the bed, sucking contentedly. He was all right. As long as he was near her. That's all he needed, really. It was perfectly simple.

Nothing else was, though. What a day! She still couldn't decide what to think about Will. She'd have to talk to someone about it. Becky. No, Colleen. If she phoned. Or maybe she could go round to her place in Ashton on Monday, after Vicky had been. Vicky might even give her a lift. And she must think about what Dad was saying. Come up with some sort of a plan. Something to get him off her back. But not now, she was much too tired. Couldn't think about anything.

# CHAPTER SEVENTEEN

'So what did Vicky say, then?' Colleen asked.

'Well, she talked a bit about my dad – she must have had a long talk with him earlier, because she seemed to know everything about him and Julie – and then she gave me these leaflets about benefits, and she tried to talk about college courses, and she asked me questions about what I wanted to do. Again.'

Colleen stopped patting Zak's hands together, pat-a-cake, to ask, 'And what *do* you want to do, Mia?'

'*I dunno!*' they chorused together, laughing. It felt so much better, laughing.

Colleen swung Isaac above her head and then back to her face, kissing his nose. He smiled and chirruped back at her.

'Perhaps you should run away to the fair with me!'

'What? You're not going? Not you, too?'

'Too?'

Mia blushed.

'Come on, Mia, who else is leaving?'

'No one really. Only Will's got a holiday job up at Mill Cove. And Becky's going on holiday with her family for three weeks to France, and Dad's probably going away with Julie.'

'Is that where you were? On Saturday? With Will?'

Mia gave Colleen the edited highlights. She played down the argument and the silent journey back to Whitecross.

Colleen sighed. 'I don't know, Mia.'

'What?'

'You put too much on to him.'

'What do you mean?'

'He's not going to be the answer, Mia.'

'You haven't even met him!' Mia was indignant.

'But he's not ready, is he?'

'What do you mean?'

'He's just not ready for you and Kai. He's still a boy, really.'

'He's the same age as me!'

'Yes, and you know what it's like, with a baby and everything. Can you really see him helping?'

Mia pictured him making the fire on the beach, whittling the sticks with the penknife he kept in his pocket; Will climbing the rocks at Mill Cove, oblivious to time, and her, and Kai, caught up in his own world. She sighed.

'I know it sounds hopeless from what I told you, but if you met him, you'd think differently.'

'Maybe. Oh, Mia, don't be miserable.'

'I am miserable. It feels like no one's on my side, not even you. And now you're talking about leaving,' Mia said. 'I didn't think it would be so soon. You can't! I need you here!'

'I've had the all clear from the hospital. I'm better. So I can join Mum. The fair's stopping for the summer somewhere on the coast. Hang on and I'll find her letter.'

Colleen rummaged through papers and books stacked on the floor in small piles.

'What are all those books for?' Mia asked. '*The Tree Book*?'

'I joined the library. There's something about that tree in your garden – the ash. It has healing properties. And the sap makes babies strong. Honest!'

Mia smiled. 'Oh, yeah?'

She looked around the room while Colleen sorted through the piles of stuff. It was dark, with cheap second-hand furniture and a brown carpet. But Colleen had done her best to liven it up with a bright red rug and tall candles in blue glass bottles. She'd put flowers in a jug on the table and over the couch had draped a green Indian bedspread with sequins and beads and tiny pieces of glass sewn into the fabric which caught and magnified the light from the window.

On the bed lay a black case with beautiful silver clasps. It was the most expensive-looking object in the entire room.

'What's this?' Mia went over and stroked the case. 'Can I open it?'

Colleen glanced up from her pile of letters. 'What? Oh, yes. It's my fiddle case.'

The violin was a rich russet wood, smooth and cool to touch. Mia lightly ran her finger over the strings and they gave a little shiver.

'Is it yours? Do you play, then?'

Will, on the beach at Whitecross: *We need a fiddle player. Do you know anyone?*

'Here it is! They'll be there week after next. Mum's sending me some money for the train. "Change at Bristol," she says here. It's by the sea, a sandy beach.' She waved the letter at Mia.

The spidery handwriting on lined paper made Mia feel even more miserable. Up till now, Colleen's mother had been a vague figure with no substance, even though Colleen talked about her so lovingly. The writing made her real. And so different, suddenly, from Mia's own mother, with her typed letters and her efficient e-mails. How different they were, really, she and Colleen.

'Why don't you come, too?' Colleen said.

'There wouldn't be room. Would there? In any case, Dad wouldn't let me.' *Do us all a favour*, when she'd first told him about her new friend. 'I wish you'd stay,' Mia said.

'We might be back in Ashton for the bank holiday. Late August. That's what usually happens with the fair. And you can visit us, can't you? Stay over for a little while at least.'

Mia didn't reply. She watched Colleen lay Isaac back on the rug, take the block of resin out of the case, rub it over the strings of the bow. She picked up the violin and tucked it under her chin.

'So you *can* play.'

Colleen smiled, twisted her long hair back over her shoulder, turned slightly towards the window and ran the bow over the strings.

Mia felt her spine shiver and uncurl. The first notes dropped into the room like tears. Isaac watched his mother intently while she played. Kai lay still on the rug on the floor where Mia had left him, his head turned to one side, listening. The sound changed; no longer sad, the tune danced and spun the notes, faster and faster.

Abruptly Colleen stopped, turned, grinned. 'Enough of that.'

'Don't stop! You're amazing.' Mia's voice was

quiet. 'Why didn't you say before that you could play like that?'

Colleen just laughed again.

'You should do something with a talent like that,' Mia said. 'You could make money. Busking on the streets, you know, like those blokes with guitars who are always down the precinct. Only you're about a thousand times better.'

'I don't want to do it for money,' Colleen said. 'I keep it for me, my playing.'

This would be the moment, Mia thought, to tell her about Will's band needing a player. But she didn't. She thought of how Colleen might look through Will's eyes and it stopped her.

That would be the last straw, to find him fancying Colleen. She felt mean about it afterwards. Maybe it would have made Colleen want to stay. That, and the garden at Whitecross, and her and Kai.

'What shall we do today?' Colleen asked her, when she'd closed the clasps on the violin case.

'I don't know. I'm so tired.'

'I can't stay in here much longer,' Colleen said. 'Got to get some air.'

'The park, then? Or the river?'

It was hard to keep thinking of things to do which didn't involve spending money.

'What about that walk along the canal? The towpath?'

'OK. Get your stuff together.'

They pushed the babies into town along the main Ashton road. The pavement was too narrow for them to walk side by side, so they walked separately, without talking. It seemed so dreary, this part of town. It made her almost glad she lived in Whitecross. Kai, in his buggy, seemed so close to the car fumes that pumped out incessantly from the slow-moving traffic. No wonder so many babies got asthma, breathing this muck in every day into their tiny, newly formed lungs.

They stopped in the precinct to sit a while on a bench. Colleen's feet ached. Her new flip-flops had rubbed her toes raw.

'I'll take them off for a bit. Go barefoot.'

She was wearing a thin red cotton skirt today and had tied her hair back with a purple scarf. Even with her bare feet and the wonky old pram she looked striking. Mia studied their reflection in the big shop windows as they walked past: her own spiky short hair, new jeans, belt: Colleen's wild hair, bright colours. Together, the two of them with their babies made people turn, stare. They pretended not to notice.

There were the usual boats moored along the canal

bank. These were the boats that stayed all year, not holiday people cruising the canals for fun. Thin dogs dozed on the towpath, soaking up the sun; they lifted their heads as Mia and Colleen walked past. A swan and four grey cygnets with huge webbed feet preened themselves on the grassy bank.

'Look at that! A tree on a boat!' Colleen laughed, pointing out the tree in its huge pot weighing down the bow of a dilapidated narrowboat. 'It's even got a bird feeder on it!'

'You laugh at everything,' Mia said.

'Because I'm happy. I'm seeing my mum in just ten days.' She danced along the path for a bit, wiggling the pram.

'Won't it be all cramped up in a caravan, though?'

'Yes, but we can be outside most of the time. Everyone hangs out together in the field, like I told you. You'd love it, Mia.'

Mia thought of the travellers she'd seen once, camped up on the grass verge next to the dual carriageway. It did look fun, on a sunny day, anyway: families hanging out together, and the dogs, and the children, and the fires. But not in some crummy old litter-strewn field next to the funfair, with the constant hum of the electric generators and traffic all night. Perhaps Colleen had her own fantasy of what things would be like, just as Mia did.

'Your mum will be working, won't she?' Mia said.

'Yes. And I can help, and she can help me. She won't believe how much Zak's changed since she saw him. He'll look huge!'

*Hardly*, Mia thought, although she didn't say so to Colleen. Kai was so much bigger than Isaac now. And stronger, too. Zak's head was still floppy, while Kai could support his already.

They walked further along the towpath. Quite quickly it felt as though they had left the town behind. A line of trees on either side of the canal screened off the backs of houses, the railway line, the busy main road. Wild comfrey and meadowsweet grew among the rushes at the edge of the canal. Colleen identified the flowers for Mia.

'And the tall pink ones like spears are rosebay willowherb. I love that name!'

On the opposite bank a break in the trees revealed a square of rough field where two large piebald horses grazed. They lifted their heads and whinnied and then ran the length of their field.

'Look!' Colleen said. 'Proper Roma horses. See their big feet?'

'Can you ride?' Mia asked.

'No. Well, we never had horses. Not many travellers do these days. They're beautiful, aren't they?'

They watched them for a while. The horses ran for

the sheer joy of it, manes and tails streaming out, free. Every so often they stopped, touched noses, whinnied, then off they ran again.

Mia's eyes filled with tears.

'What's the matter, Mia?'

'I'm just fed up with everything. I'm tired out. And yet everyone talks as if I ought to be doing more. No one seems to understand that it's more than enough for me, just looking after Kai properly. Why does everyone go on and on about what I'm going to do, as if I'm not already doing anything? It's as if looking after Kai doesn't count.'

'They've forgotten what it's like.'

'If they ever knew. Dad was at work all day when I was a baby. He didn't see what it was like. And Vicky's this super-capable person who can do millions of things at the same time, like work and have a child and study for exams. But I'm not like that.'

'What about your mum, though?'

'She's just blotted the whole thing out, I reckon, it was so awful. And she's scared about me, I think.'

'Why?'

'I dunno. Like, what's going to happen to me? If I don't have exams and a good job and all that.'

'She wouldn't think much of my mum, then. She's never passed an exam in her life. Nor me.'

Colleen parked up her pram by a wooden bench.

'But we still have a good life! We can have a laugh and a good time. We don't have much money, that's all.'

'But you've got each other. You really love your mum.'

'Yes, and you've got your dad, haven't you?'

'Yes, but it's not the same. It's like he's had enough of being my dad. And he loves Kai to bits, but he's too busy working to help much. And he wants Julie now.'

They sat together on the bench. Both babies slept peacefully.

Colleen squeezed Mia's arm. 'Poor you. But you've got to remember there's lots of different ways of being a mother.'

Mia sighed.

She was remembering again the letter Mum had sent her last year, when she thought Mia was going to have an abortion. *It would be for the best*, she'd said. Mia could get her exams and then she could really *spread her wings and fly*.

But Mia had chosen to keep the baby. Mum's words had filled her with rage. She hadn't understood what Mum had meant at the time. It was becoming clearer to her now.

'Mum didn't want me to have the baby,' Mia said.

Colleen looked utterly shocked. It would be

unimaginable for her own mother to think something like that.

'I think she wishes she hadn't had us, really.'

'No, don't say that. Stop it, Mia. You're getting yourself in a right state. Just enjoy being here now. Make the most of it. It all changes so fast. Everything will be all right, you'll see.'

*Everything will be all right*. Mia used to say that. Drifting along, just expecting everything to sort itself out. But it didn't seem enough any more. It seemed that everyone else's life was changing, moving on. And she was stuck.

They sat for a while in silence, soaking up the sun.

Mia eventually stood up. 'I'm too hot. And thirsty. And I'm really tired today. I'm going back.'

'OK. I'll stay here a bit longer.'

'Do you want to come over? Wednesday?'

'I've got to go to the clinic Wednesday, get Zak weighed. Vicky said.'

'Thursday, then? Friday?'

'Friday. I'll come to your house, shall I?'

Mia leaned down, hugged Colleen briefly. 'Thanks.'

She couldn't bear to think Colleen would be leaving so soon. Just when she'd found her.


Thursday. Mia had forgotten that it was the last GCSE exam that morning. Maths Paper Two. The

Whitecross crowd were all at the bus station, waiting for the bus home.

Becky waved enthusiastically. 'Mia! What are you doing here? Ah, look at Kai! Doesn't he look sweet! I like his stars and fishes!' She gave them a little twirl. 'Shall I help you with the buggy?'

Liam and Matt and Will stood back slightly. Will had gone bright red. Becky held the sleepy baby while Mia folded up the buggy. It was easy now she'd done it so often.

'We're off down the beach for a celebration,' Becky said. 'You can come, too! Brilliant! Tasha's coming in a minute – she's gone to the supermarket to get stuff.'

It used to be her, getting the drink. Only she'd got caught too often – underage.

Mia glanced at Will. He was watching her; he nodded slightly.

Why shouldn't she join in? They were her friends, too.

Tasha staggered over to the bus stop with clinking carrier bags in both hands.

'Mia!' She put down the bags, hugged her. 'I didn't know you were coming!'

'It's only by chance,' Mia said. 'Otherwise I wouldn't have known. Like Saturday.'

Tasha pulled a face. 'Sorry. It was just a spur of the moment thing, you know? We've really finished!

Do you realize, everybody? We're free!' Tasha gave a squawk of delight.

Becky clucked at Kai. 'He's really looking at everyone now, isn't he? Taking it all in.'

On the bus, the three girls took it in turns to hold him. Will, Matt and Liam sat together at the back. Will stumbled forwards as they approached their stop and lifted the buggy out of the luggage compartment.

'I'll take this,' he muttered.

He fumbled with the catches, trying to put it up on the pavement. Matt and Liam laughed.

'You try, then, if you think it's so funny,' Will said.

'Give it here. I'll do it,' Mia said.

'Why don't we carry Kai,' Tasha said, 'and put all the bottles and food and stuff in the buggy?'

'Brilliant. Let me hold Kai.' Becky took him from Tasha.

Mia watched anxiously from behind as Becky crossed the main road with her baby. His little face peeped back at her over Becky's shoulder.

'All right?' Matt asked Mia.

She nodded.

It got easier once they'd all had a few drinks. It was almost like old times, back being part of the crowd. But she couldn't drink as much as the rest of them.

The alcohol would get in her milk, she knew, and she couldn't do that to Kai. It would be like poisoning him. The conversation started to seem less funny. Too much talk about school, and results, and next September. A levels. Holiday jobs. And there was no way she was going to breastfeed Kai in front of Liam and Matt, so she had to leave the beach before all the others.

Becky went with her as far as the footpath.

'You OK? You seem a bit down? Quieter than usual.'

'I'm just not pissed like the rest of you.'

'Will you be all right by yourself?'

'Of course. I'm used to it.'

Sarcasm was wasted on Becky.

'See you soon, then! Bye!'

Becky ran back to rejoin the others and Mia went on alone.

The house seemed even quieter and more lonely than usual. She put the telly on while she fed Kai in the sitting room. Load of rubbish, daytime telly. Kai seemed restless, he didn't want to sleep. He arched his back and cried angrily each time she tried to lay him down in the basket. She wandered round the garden with him over her arm, like she'd seen other mothers do. It felt oppressively hot; clouds were beginning to build up. There were too many flies, tiny biting ones. She went back inside, drifted about the house, showing Kai things as if she were Colleen.

'This is the clock. See. And here's a photograph of your aunties, Laura and Kate, who are off having a wonderful time at university, and travelling, and don't care about us one little bit. And here's a photo of your granny.'

Kai squirmed in her arms. She'd been standing still too long, examining the photograph. It was one of Mum when she was much younger, holding Laura as a baby. Mia pored over her face, trying to read the expression. She didn't look elated, or beatific, or brimful of joy, like mothers were supposed to look. She looked tired, and strained, and distant, as if she wasn't quite there. She looked like Mia.

Mia's mobile phone rang. She picked it up, heard giggling.

'Becky?'

'Hi, Mia!' Giggle. 'Just checking you're OK!' Giggle.

'Oh, Becks! You're completely pissed.'

'And we want you to know – that we think Kai's gorgeous and just like Will – and you're very lucky – and Will's playing at the pub on Friday and we're all going, and we want you to –'

'Stop it, Becky.' Mia's throat ached with suppressed sobs. 'Call me when you've sobered up.'

She turned off her phone.

Mia lay on her bed, Kai wide awake at her side. The cat was stretched out on the duvet, shedding ginger hairs everywhere, but she let him stay. She picked up the paperback from the bedside cabinet and tried reading a bit more of the first chapter. It was about three girls sliding down sand dunes, and the writing was beautiful, but she couldn't concentrate on the words. She kept thinking about Laura in Bristol, and Kate, somewhere in Turkey now, and Becky and everyone making plans for the summer and next year.

That letter from Mum: *You've got your whole life ahead of you.*

She leaned out of bed and rummaged through the piles of dusty papers in the cabinet, hunting for it. Instead, she came across the old notebook she used to write in last year, when she was pregnant.

She lay back on the bed, notebook open on the pillow, and started to read.

## CHAPTER EIGHTEEN

*I*t was strange, reading her own handwriting. To begin with, it didn't seem like it was her at all. But step by step, it took her back.

*October 14th. Week ten, and already it's decided whether it's a boy or a girl. Little Bean, growing inside me. She (I think it must be a girl, because I can only imagine someone like me, though very tiny, 4.5 cm to be exact) has fingers and toes already, too. I haven't told Will about what happened at the hospital. I'll have to tell him. He's a right to know. He'll be a father, and nothing can change that.*

The usual blackbird was in the top of the tree. She watched it through the open window. A male bird, glossy and black. The female, with its drab brown, raggedy feathers, was scurrying about the lawn, pecking amongst the leaves, searching out food for the fledglings in the nest.

She turned another page in the notebook. She'd written in it after she'd got back home, and her mum had come down to Whitecross and told her all about what it had been like for her, having young children, being pregnant. Why she'd left, when Mia was so little ... *she said maybe it was a healing thing for me, having this baby. And that I could be a much better mother than she had been. I bloody hope so.*

Beside her, Kai kicked and smiled and held out his hand to the strip of sunlight shining on to the edge of the bed. Above them both, the silver stars circled gently in the warm air currents.

*Sunday. Went down to the sea really early, before anyone was up. Snow everywhere still, even on the beach. I've never seen that before.*

*The sky was a pale, delicate blue. Baby Blue. And a thin sliver of moon floated just above the horizon. Today I'm full of hope and excitement about the baby. I know we're going to be all right, Little Bean and me. I'm really going to try.*

Mia turned over the next page in the notebook. No more entries; she'd not written another word. But a small white feather drifted out from between the pages. She must have stuck it in there, between the blank pages, for safe keeping.

She picked it up carefully. It was still soft. She brushed it against her cheek.

*Soft as a newborn baby's downy head.*

Mia looked at Kai, snuggled beside her on the bed. The fluff of his dark hair. Her hair, but softer, finer. She stroked it smooth and he turned towards her. He could do that now, turn his head where he wanted it. Each day there were new things. Small things that no one but a mother would notice. Small, important things.

She watched him for a long time.

Mia rummaged in the bedside cabinet again, searching for a pen. She found her old pencil case from school, still smelling of dusty classrooms, and pencil sharpenings, and spearmint gum. She chose a black pen, extra fine, smoothed the clean notebook page open, and began to write.

*June 29th. He's lying beside me now. He. Because Little Bean turns out to be Kai. Today he's wearing his turquoise Babygro from Becky and a blue cardigan with yellow fish buttons – Will's mum knitted it for him. His dark hair's all fine and wispy. There's a patch at the back where it's almost worn away, but it'll grow back again, Vicky says. His eyes are a deep blue, like Will's. Celtic colouring, Dad says, like his name. Kai's changed so much in just seven weeks. Gradually, he's opening out. Like a flower that starts off as a tight bud. He lies on his back and he can turn his head now, and he reaches out with his hand. Opens the fingers like a starfish. Or shuts them tight, clamped round my finger, a limpet.*

Her hand began to ache from gripping the pen so tightly. The writing was messy, but it flowed out of her. Now she'd started, she couldn't stop.

*He is completely beautiful and perfect, and when I look at him sometimes I can't believe that he came from me. Because he is so much himself. And there's this feeling inside me I can't describe. Sometimes it feels as if I'll burst with it. Warm, and quivering, and alive. I think it's love. I see it on Colleen's face when she's looking at Isaac and she can't stop smiling. It sounds corny, talking about love like that. But it isn't. It's the most amazing thing. I didn't know that I could feel like this.*

As she wrote, she felt the magic, the miracle of the baby somehow being restored. It was as if she were coming back into herself, remembering something so important about why she'd chosen to keep him in the first place, even before she really knew who he was.

The wind outside in the garden had got up. It rattled the window, blew gusts that jangled and twisted the strings of stars dangling from the dark blue ceiling. The first splatter of rain struck the window.

She lay and listened to it drumming on the glass, the softer sounds of rain on leaves. The cat curled itself round more tightly next to her feet. Kai still lay with his eyes open, watching the movement of the leaves of the ash tree. She stroked his cheek for a while and soon his eyes began to close. He flickered them open again, once, twice, three times, as if he were checking she was still there, before he let himself fall completely asleep.

Mia felt a deep peace spreading through her tired body. She didn't sleep; she stayed watching over her sleeping child, taking in all over again the miracle of him.

Dad's key in the lock. She'd forgotten she was supposed to be cooking supper tonight. Mia slipped out from beside Kai, wedged him safely on the middle of the bed with pillows, lifted the cat and took him with her downstairs.

'Hello, Dad. You're late.'

'Sorry, love. Everything OK?'

'What are those?'

Dad dumped a pile of glossy magazines on the kitchen table. He flushed. 'Holiday brochures.'

'Oh? And?'

'We thought of taking a week or two away.'

'We?'

'Julie and I.'

Mia leafed through the brochures. *The Magic of Italy. Romantic Greece. Hidden Spain.*

'I should have said something before, I know.' Dad was flustered. 'But I thought I'd wait till it was more definite. Sorry.'

'It's OK, Dad. I don't mind.'

'You don't? Blimey. "The Times They Are A-Changin'"! Bob Dylan,' he added, 'in case you didn't know.'

'Well, just a bit before my time, Dad.' She smiled. 'And Julie's, for that matter.'

'You're in a good mood. What's happened?'

'Don't know. Just feeling better, somehow.'

'Good.' Dad kissed the top of her head. 'You're doing a great job, you know? As a mum, I mean. I know it's not easy. But he's the best, that baby of yours. My grandson!' He wrinkled up his nose. 'Only that makes me sound so old.'

'Well, you are.'

'Thanks, Mia.'

'Any time, Dad.'

He smiled. He looked tired. 'Supper nearly ready?'

'Sorry. I forgot. I haven't even started it. I'll do something quick.'

'I'll have a drink, then, and a bath. Where is Kai?'

'Sleeping. Just gone off.'

Mia put on a saucepan for pasta and started chopping up onions and garlic. People said you shouldn't eat spicy stuff if you were breastfeeding, but Kai didn't seem to mind. He was growing and putting on weight exactly as he should. She wondered briefly how Colleen had got on at the clinic with Zak. She'd find out tomorrow. She hoped it wouldn't be bad news, nothing serious. He hardly seemed to be growing at all. Poor Colleen. No wonder she wanted her mum.

From upstairs came the sound of Dad singing loudly in his bath. 'Mr Tambourine Man'. On to his complete Bob Dylan repertoire now. She hoped he wouldn't wake Kai. But it was nice to hear him singing, sounding happy. The whole atmosphere in the house had lifted.

Mia coiled spaghetti into the boiling water. 'Nine minutes!' she yelled upstairs.

It was because of her that it had changed, wasn't it? Something had shifted.

## CHAPTER NINETEEN

Mia woke in the night to hear thunder. It rumbled in the distance, rolled closer. She found herself counting the spaces between the lightning and the sound, like she used to as a little girl. Kai stirred in his basket but did not wake up. The lightning illuminated the whole room, cast strange shadows. But she wasn't frightened, not like she used to be.

She'd had this recurring dream, as a child, about Dad being struck by lightning and turning to stone. In the dream, she found his body stretched out in the garden, a stone effigy like you see in old cathedrals, hands together as if in prayer. She supposed that was what she'd dreaded throughout her childhood: that something would happen to him, too, and she'd be left totally alone. That was how important he was. He'd been there when mum had left, and he still was, in his own way, even though it was all changing now. *Children need fathers.* That was what Becky had said, and it was true. It was true for her, wasn't it? And so it must be true for Kai, too.

Mia lay in the dark, thinking about Will. Colleen had been right when she said he wasn't ready yet, but he still might be. She'd have to take it one step at a time. Build up their friendship again. Perhaps she'd try and go to see him play with his band at the pub with Becky and the others. Dad might babysit Kai for an hour. Or Becky's mum.

She could take an interest in his music, like she used to. Perhaps she could get Colleen to teach her how to play something. That violin, snug in its beautiful velvet-lined case. Or something a bit easier to begin with, like the piano. May be she could learn to sing.

Colleen would be over in the morning. Mia thought again about little Isaac not growing properly. Maybe it was simply because Colleen wasn't really happy, wasn't thriving, away from her mum and her people. Maybe she did need to go and live with her mother for the summer. But even if she did, she still might be persuaded to come back and stay with Mia for two weeks while Dad and Julie went away. And then – Mia was getting quite carried away now – when he saw how well she and Colleen got on, and how responsible she was getting now, Dad might agree that it would be a very good idea for Mia and Colleen and the babies to get a flat together in the autumn. Not a flat, Mia corrected herself. It would have to be a house, with a garden and a tree. Colleen couldn't thrive without a garden, and the babies needed one, too.

It was a good plan, wasn't it? A start, at least. She would talk to Colleen about it in the morning.

Colleen could go and visit her mum whenever she needed to. Mia might even visit hers in Bristol. And the house in Whitecross would still be here, for her to come back to. Even if Julie was there, too. Becky and Tasha would still be around. They'd babysit, sometimes. And all the mothers – Becky's, and Will's even.

Mia felt too excited to sleep.

She saw the first faint flush of light in the sky. This time of year it came so early. She watched the pale splash of colour begin to spread. Then came the first notes of a bird. And another, and others began to join in.

Now the garden was full of birdsong. It was as if the feeling she had held in her all night, a sort of pent-up joy, was being released at last. She wanted to join in, too, her voice to sing out with all the others.

From the ivy-clad wall came a great chirping and

scuffling, and then the warning sound of the male blackbird as he flew to the tree. Mia watched as, one by one, the fledglings fluttered from the nest, from wall to hedge and back again. She counted them. Four.

Where was the cat? He'd been watching them for days now. But last night's storm had kept him inside; he'd missed his moment. For now, the baby birds were safe.

Now. This moment. That was how you had to think of it. This moment was all you ever had, this, and the next, and the next. *Make the most of it*, Colleen had said. *It all changes so fast*. But it didn't mean you couldn't plan, and think about what might come next.

Now the sky was full of light. After all the rain and wind in the night, the air felt washed clean, the garden greener and more vivid. Cream petals from the climbing rose lay scattered across the grass. The leaves of the ash tree rustled together.

What had Colleen's tree book called it, the ash tree? 'The tree of rebirth and healing'. The leaves of the ash tree were believed to bring good luck; the sap protected newborn babies and made them strong.

Mia smiled. Mum had loved that tree when she lived here. It was there in the photograph on the chest of drawers, the one where Mum held little Mia on her lap. She'd collected seeds from the tree to plant in her new garden, the one in Bristol. Each year there were thousands of seeds, each one with the potential for a new, full-sized tree tucked inside.

Dad and Mia had breakfast together early, before he left for work. Kai bounced in his chair on the table as they ate toast.

'He'll bounce right off that soon, if we're not careful! We'll have to get him one of those things you hang from the door frame. You know? So he can bounce from the floor.'

'I've been thinking, Dad.'

'Yes?'

'About what you said the other night. About you and Julie and everything.'

'And?' He carried on eating, pretending not to be tense in every muscle. She could see his hand gripping the mug.

'Well, I was thinking, maybe I'd try and find a place to live with Colleen. So we can sign on for a college course in the autumn, or after Christmas, maybe.'

'You don't have to move out of here,' Dad said. His face was red. 'I wasn't trying to push you out.'

'No, I think it would be good. We'd help each other, Colleen and me. With the babies. And with studying. That's if I can persuade her. And Kai and

I, well, we could still come here lots, at weekends and that, couldn't we?'

Dad frowned. 'You're only just sixteen. It's very young to leave home.'

'So? I can look after myself, can't I? And Kai. You said how well I was doing.'

'Yes, but – well, that's completely different. That's with you living here. What would you do at college, anyway?'

'Get some exams. GCSEs. Might as well. I'm not stupid.'

'I know you're not. You know I've never thought that. Lazy, maybe. Easily distracted. But that was before you had Kai. You've grown up a lot, these last couple of months. You've had to. But what would you do for money? Benefits won't be enough to live on, you know.'

'Mum said she'd help out with money, didn't she? While I'm at college, at least. Later, I can get a part-time job. If I can get some exams, I can get a better job.'

'My God! Never thought I'd hear those words coming out of your mouth, Mia Kitson! So you have been listening all these years!'

'Dad! Don't spoil it now.'

'OK, sorry. But this Colleen – she's not going to want to stay in one place, is she?'

'She might. She's loved coming here these last few weeks, the garden and that. I'm going to ask her. See what she says. So you can go ahead and make your plans with Julie.'

Dad looked sheepish. 'We've already started, actually, making plans. The holiday's booked. Two weeks in August. I thought Laura might be able to come back and stay here with you then. But maybe you'd like to ask your friend instead. Colleen.'

He stood up, scraped toast crusts into the bin, put the plate into the washing-up bowl.

'Got to be off. Year Twelves, first thing. *The Tempest*: themes of loss and redemption. But thank you, Mia. For thinking about it all. Makes a huge difference to me. Talk more later, yes?' He hugged her as he went past, out of the room, blew a kiss at Kai.

'One last thing.' She stood in the doorway as he carried his box of school books to the car. 'Would you and Julie be able to babysit Kai tonight? So I can go out to hear Will's band play? Just for an hour or two?'

Dad crinkled his eyebrows, grinned. 'Of course. Delighted.'

She watched him drive off. The radio blared out full volume. Radio 2. Honestly!

*

Kai smiled up at Mia as she carried him in his bouncy chair into the sitting room. He chirruped at her: a new sound.

Mia smiled back at him. 'Are you talking to me, Birdy?'

She opened the French windows so he could see out into the garden while she rummaged through the stack of ancient LPs that Dad kept under the desk in the corner. *Greatest Hits*. She got the record out of the paper sleeve, put it on the stereo that Dad had fixed up on top of the CD player. Funny to think these records were all they'd had, back when Dad was her age.

She found the track: 'It's All Over Now Baby Blue'. Turned up the volume. Then she played the whole record. Dad would've been proud of her!

'What the hell is that?'

Colleen stood at the open French windows, Isaac in his sling on her front, laughing at Mia singing along to Dad's old record.

Mia turned the volume down. 'Dad's,' she explained.

'Why were you listening to it, then?'

'Just for fun. It's not bad, actually.'

'Sounded terrible to me.' Colleen stepped from the garden into the sitting room and flopped down on the sofa to untie the sling.

'You're earlier than I expected.'

'Obviously.'

'Is everything OK?'

'Yes. No. I don't know.' Colleen's eyes filled with tears.

'What's happened?'

'The clinic. Vicky. They're worried about Zak now. I'm better, but they say he's much too little. So now I've got to go and take him to the hospital for tests.'

'Oh, Colleen, I'm sorry.'

'Mum's going to come up. I've spoken to her. She'll come to the hospital with me.'

'It probably isn't anything,' Mia said. 'They're just being careful.'

Colleen held Zak on her lap. His dark eyes followed the movement of the leaves outside.

'I've got to feed him more. I thought I might borrow that book you said about, ages ago, about starting to breastfeed again.' She got a bottle of formula milk out of her bag. 'Can I warm this up for him?'

While they waited for the kettle to boil, Mia started to tell Colleen about her plan.

'It might fit in,' she said. 'You might be able to stay here while Dad's away, mightn't you? Please? Just two weeks? As long as Zak's OK?'

'I'll think about it,' Colleen said.

'What do they think is wrong with Zak?'

'They didn't say. Just said they need to do some tests. He's small, that's all, really. I'd know if there was something really wrong with him, wouldn't I?'

'Yes. Course you would. He's bright as anything. He's been smiling for weeks. He doesn't look ill or anything. Don't worry about it.'

'I can't help it. You would, if it was Kai.'

'I know. I'm sorry. I understand. I really do.'

'I don't want to stay in today. Let's go somewhere.'

They walked down to the sea. A different sort of beach, after last night's storm, from the one they'd lazed about on for the past three weeks. There was a new line of flotsam, washed up by the high tide, mixed with a mound of stinking seaweed, and a new, higher bank of pebbles. They walked along it, kicking bottles and bits of driftwood.

Colleen started picking up bits of nylon fishing rope that had been washed up: all different colours, orange and bright blue and green. She found a piece of wood, held it up and turned it round till it made a shape a bit like a horse. She made it a mane and tail with frayed strands of rope.

Mia hunkered down beside her.

'Make one for Kai, too. Please.'

'Not a horse, something else. This piece, look. It's a swan. Or maybe a goose.' She held up a piece of wood, softened and sculpted by the sea. There was the curve of a head, and a beak, and a hole where an eye might be. 'If we had something sharp, then we could carve feathers on the wings.'

'It should be a seabird for Kai.'

'Whatever.'

The sea was flat and grey today. Even the birds sounded sad and mournful, flying low over the water, calling. Colleen was unusually subdued. Preoccupied with Isaac, presumably. She kept trying to feed him from his bottle, but he turned his head away, dribbled milk out of his mouth as if he had already had too much.

'Perhaps he'd like it better if it was warmed up?'

Colleen frowned.

'I know you can't, here. Do you want to go back home?'

Colleen shook her head. 'No way. I need to be outside. And I love it here.' She smiled at Mia. She'd got her dreamy look. 'What this beach needs is a cafe.'

'No one would go to a cafe here. It's not that sort of beach.'

'We would. Us and the babies. And those people you know from school.'

Mia laughed. 'You couldn't run a cafe on that! You need holiday people. And they all go further up the coast. There's nothing here.'

'There could be. I can see it now. Our cafe. Famous for miles around.' Colleen started to cheer up. 'Cheap but classy, all at the same time. With special things for babies and children, like books and toys, and little chairs and tables the right height. And music nights on Fridays. Wild. Fiddle-playing by the cafe owner by special request!'

'It could be like a beach hut, wooden, with shutters, and a veranda,' Mia joined in.

'Painted blue.'

'Will's band could play on Saturdays. People would come from miles around to hear him playing the saxophone.'

'We could call it Cafe Blue.'

'*Bleu*.'

'Pardon?'

'Cafe Bleu. If it's a cafe, it should have a French name. *Bleu* is the French for blue.'

'OK, if you insist. And – and –'

'And in the winter we'd board it up and live in a snug little house in town.'

'No! Why can't we keep it open all year? The beach cafe that's always open. I bet the sea's beautiful in winter.'

'Not this sea! Not here in Whitecross. The smell's enough to drive you away. Rotting seaweed, washed up by storms. All the rubbish. Freezing-cold wind.'

'The trouble is, you're too real,' Colleen teased.

Zak had fallen asleep, his face squashed to one side of the sling, his little mouth half open. Colleen lay back on the damp pebbles and closed her eyes.

Mia watched her for a while. She loved the way they'd conjured up the cafe together so clearly. She could almost see it now, at the top of the beach – the wooden tables packed with people, music drifting out over the sea. Fairy lights.

'The trouble is,' she said softly, 'I don't want to stay here in Whitecross. Not forever. It's all right for you. You've travelled already. You've had sixteen years of it. I've got to get out, get going.'

Colleen opened her eyes. 'You will,' she said. 'If you want to enough. But there's loads of time. And for now we've got the babies to think of. Let's make the most of what we've got already, right now.' She looked down at her sleeping son.

She was right, of course.

Mia thought again about the excitement she'd felt all night, the sense of things starting over, of so much being possible.

'Will you think about what I said earlier, back at the house?' Mia asked Colleen. 'About us? That was for real.'

'I have been. I want to go back with Mum first, when we've finished with the hospital, but I'll come back. I'll come and stay while your dad's away, if it all fits in. And then maybe we should look for a place to share. At the end of the summer.' She turned to Mia. 'When we've done the tests and that, once I've stopped worrying about Zak, you know, I'll be really excited. Promise!'

A slight breeze ruffled the water. They watched the way it patterned the surface, a cross-hatching of silver. The grey sky was lifting, getting lighter. Above the horizon, it had already paled to a thin strip of blue.

From the far end of the beach, a single figure walked steadily towards them. So. He'd known she might be here; maybe he'd even planned to find her and Kai. Now she could introduce him to Colleen, and tell him she'd be there with Becky and the others to listen to him play tonight.

Bit by bit, the different strands of her life were weaving together.

She stood up, waved, then looked at Colleen.

'It's Will!' she said.

Mia shifted Kai up in her arms. His head turned as a thin ray of sunlight caught the shallow water, danced and sparkled on the tiny waves breaking on the pebbles. He stretched out one little hand.

Mia kissed it. 'Everything's going to be all right,' she whispered to Kai. 'Come on, let's go and meet him.'